Michael Turned Toward Isabelle. "Your Daughter Is Delightful."

Isabelle foolishly felt like crying. "You—you were very good with her."

"I like kids. I always wanted a family. I guess it's from all those years I spent bumping around from foster home to foster home. Never belonging anywhere."

There was a distant look in his eyes for a moment, and Isabelle felt a sympathetic tightening in her chest. "I remember your telling me how much you hated it."

"I always swore I'd be the best dad ever. Even when I was a teenager, I'd think about how I'd do things with my kids, teach them stuff." He shrugged. "Now here I am—never had any."

Guilt wriggled through Isabelle. *Had she been wrong to withhold Jenny from him all these years?*

Dear Reader,

For many years you have known and loved Silhouette author Robin Elliott. But did you know she is also popular romance writer Joan Elliott Pickart? Now she has chosen to write her Silhouette books using the Joan Elliott Pickart name, which is also her real name!

You'll be reading the same delightful stories you've grown to love from "Robin Elliott," only now, keep an eye out for Joan Elliott Pickart. Joan's first book using her real name is this month's *Man of the Month.* It's called *Angels and Elves,* and it's the first in her BABY BET series. What exactly is a "baby bet"? Well, you'll have to read to find out, but I assure you—it's a lot of fun!

November also marks the return to Silhouette Books of popular writer Kristin James, with her first Silhouette Desire title, *Once in a Blue Moon.* I'm thrilled that Kristin has chosen to be part of the Desire family, and I know her many fans can't wait to read this sexy love story.

Some other favorites are also in store for you this month: Jennifer Greene, Jackie Merritt and Lass Small. And a new writer is always a treat—new writers are the voices of tomorrow, after all! This month, Pamela Ingrahm makes her writing debut...and I hope we'll see many more books from this talented new author.

Until next month, happy reading!

Lucia Macro
Senior Editor

Please address questions and book requests to:
Silhouette Reader Service
U.S.: 3010 Walden Ave., P.O. Box 1325, Buffalo, NY 14269
Canadian: P.O. Box 609, Fort Erie, Ont. L2A 5X3

KRISTIN JAMES
ONCE IN A BLUE MOON

SILHOUETTE *Desire*
Published by Silhouette Books
America's Publisher of Contemporary Romance

SILHOUETTE BOOKS

ISBN 0-373-05962-0

ONCE IN A BLUE MOON

KRISTIN JAMES,

a former attorney, is married to a family counselor, and they have a young daughter. Her family and her writing keep her busy, but when she does have free time, she loves to read. In addition to her contemporary romances, she has written a number of historicals.

One

She had not expected to ever see him again.

But here he was, walking through the door with Danny Archer and Carol Nieman, all three of them smiling like Cheshire cats and talking in that light, self-satisfied way that betokened the end of a deal.

Isabelle's stomach clenched. She wanted to turn and run away, yet there was nothing she could do except stand and watch them walk across the soundstage toward her and the rest of the cast.

She recognized Michael immediately despite the fact that it had been over ten years since she'd seen him. He still walked in that intensely masculine, loose-limbed way, like an animal on the prowl; his body was still lean and powerful. And the smile flashing across his face was just as charming as ever. Charm, after all, was his stock in trade, Isabelle thought sardonically.

"Curtis Townsend," Phil Ridley murmured beside her.

"What?" Isabelle glanced at Phil, confused.

Phil nodded toward the producer and assistant producer and the man in between them, buttressed like a prize. "I'll lay you odds that he's going to play Curtis Townsend. You know, the brother they keep talking about."

"Oh." Recent scripts had been rife with references to Mark Townsend's brother, Curtis, a character who had left the show years before. There had been a great deal of speculation that the character was to be brought back.

Isabelle's stomach knotted even tighter. *Surely that could not be. Surely she was not doomed to having Michael Traynor permanently around her—in the same studio twelve hours a day, seeing him in the actor's lounge, running into him walking along the hallway, even rehearsing and acting opposite him on the set!* Panic seized her. She knew she could not bear it.

"People!" Danny Archer was speaking now into the waiting silence, smiling at the cast and crew. He loved having them all hanging on his words. "I have someone here I want you to meet. His name is Michael Traynor." His grin broadened, and he gave a jovial little laugh. "A name I'm sure you've all heard of. I'm proud to say that we have managed to woo him away from New York and that other show, which shall remain nameless." He paused for the polite murmur of laughter. "Starting next week, he is going to be our new Curtis Townsend."

Phil cast Isabelle an arch look, raising his brows. Isabelle felt sick. *How could this be happening?* She had thought Michael safe in New York, tied by his popularity in "Eden Crossing." She had blithely believed that she would never have to see him again, never have to face the past that lay between them.

"Let me introduce you to your castmates, Michael," Danny continued, propelling Michael forward with a hand on his elbow. "Of course, Lena you already know."

Michael smiled, reaching out to take her hand. "Yes. Thank you again for reading with me in the audition."

Lena almost simpered. "It was a pleasure." Obviously Michael hadn't lost a bit of his charm, Isabelle thought sourly.

"This is Paul Kusorka—he plays Chase Manning. And Vivian Blair..."

They were proceeding down the line, coming ever closer to her. Isabelle knew that she would have to meet Michael face-to-face. She steeled herself. She must not let him realize how much seeing him again shook her. She would not let him have that power over her, that satisfaction.

Another thought struck her: *Would he even remember her? Recognize her?* It had been ten years, after all, and she was well aware of how much less important that summer had been to *him* than it had been to her. It would be a relief, of course, if he looked at her without recognition, with the vague, indeterminate charm of a new acquaintance—but how humiliating, as well. A painful reminder of the fact that she had been nothing but a summer fling for him, easily forgotten when he returned to New York.

She raised her chin, assuming a cool expression. She was determined not to let her face reflect any response to him, whether he remembered her or not. She would be aloof, remote, unaffected by him.

Danny and Michael were two people away now, chatting with Lyle Gordon, the director. Isabelle waited, surreptitiously wiping her sweating palm against her skirt.

Michael glanced away from Lyle and his eyes moved to Phil, then to Isabelle. She felt the full force of his magnetic blue gaze. It was hard to hide the involuntary quiver that ran through her. *God, he was handsome.*

Distant memory could not prepare her for the power of his looks. He was older now, the thick black hair shorter and tamed into a more conservative style, as befitted the upright doctor that Curtis Townsend was supposed to be. But the lines in his face only added interest to his smooth good looks, the added flesh removing some of the gauntness of his prominent facial bones. His eyes held a more haunting look of experience and wisdom.

There was none of the surprise in his face that Isabelle had felt when she saw him enter the room. But there was no blankness, either; he knew her, and he had known that she would be here. Then he must have recognized her name when Danny or Carol had told him about the other cast members. Or perhaps he'd even noticed that she was on "All Our Tomorrows" before he had auditioned for the part. Obviously it made no difference to him that she was on the show. But, then, she told herself, she didn't know why she should expect that it would. Michael Traynor no doubt felt no pain at the mention of her name; he would not flinch at the idea of working with her. A brief summer affair would not loom large in his past.

Now they were standing in front of her, and Danny was saying her name. Isabelle forced herself to smile and extend her hand to Michael. She felt so stiff, she thought her cheeks might crack.

"Hello."

"Isabelle."

"You two know each other?" Archer asked in surprise.

"Yes. We know each other." Michael smiled faintly, looking into Isabelle's face. His hand was warm around hers. She realized that she remembered exactly how his skin felt.

"We met a long time ago," Isabelle explained coolly to Danny, "at a summer theater." She turned to Michael, gazing challengingly into his eyes, willing herself not to notice their disturbing blueness. "I'm surprised that you remember me."

Michael's dark, straight brows went up at that statement. "I could hardly forget you," he said simply.

She wished that she could say that she had forgotten him, but, of course, it would be too rude, as well as untrue. How could she forget him, when everyday she found herself looking into that same face when she gazed at her daughter?

"Of course not," Danny agreed, grinning. "Who could forget a woman who looks like you, Isabelle?"

Isabelle gave him a perfunctory smile. "Thank you, Danny. Let's just hope the viewers don't."

Behind Michael, Carol Nieman, laughed. "Hardly likely. You're everyone's favorite villainess, and you know it." She cast a roguish glance at Michael. "Isabelle's our resident man-eater, you see—Jessica Randall."

Michael nodded. "I know."

"Yes, of course. She's devouring your character's brother at the moment."

Michael smiled at Isabelle slightly and released her hand. She hadn't realized that he had continued to hold it until that moment; her hand was a little empty and cold now.

"I look forward to working with you."

"Oh, I doubt we'll have many scenes together," Isabelle replied breezily, turning and walking away from Michael without waiting to see his expression.

She strode through the increasing crowd on the set, smiling and nodding at people, trying to look calm and unconcerned, as if she were just strolling back to her dressing room. As if she were not running away.

Isabelle closed the door of her dressing room behind her and collapsed heavily into the chair in front of her mirror. She leaned her elbows upon the vanity and rested her head on her hands.

How could this have happened? It seemed the most appalling trick of fate. She had long ago dismissed the fear that she might meet Michael again. Why, it had been years since she had even thought about him—at least in any more than a brief, passing way. And now, to have him turn up, here on her set....

For a moment she panicked and thought of running, of packing up and taking Jenny and moving away. Then she drew a long breath and forced herself to calm down. That was ridiculous; she couldn't overturn her life and run simply because an old boyfriend had appeared. And that's all he was, she reminded herself: an old boyfriend. Someone who had once, for a brief summer, had a place in her life and who no longer did.

It was not a disaster. Other women had old lovers reappear in their lives; why, here among the relatively small acting world of L.A., some women had to face their ex's all the time, even right after they had split up. At least she had had ten years for the wounds to heal before she had to face Michael again.

Isabelle raised her head and looked at herself in the mirror. She didn't like what she saw: the frown line be-

tween her eyes, the vulnerable mouth, the anxiety loom-
ing in her eyes. She looked like a victim, she thought, and
she was determined never to be that, never to think of
herself that way. Those horrible, pain-filled two years
after Michael left her were a thing of the past; she was not
the frightened, lonely girl she had been then. She had
taken control of her life; she had gone after what she
wanted; she had taken care of herself and of Jenny—so
well, in fact, that most people would be envious of her
life now.

She ought to thank Michael for what he had done, really; it had enabled her to be the person she was now.
Sometimes she wondered if she would ever have had the
strength or the nerve to have packed up and come to
L.A., to pit herself against the terrible odds of becoming a successful actress, if Michael had not left her. The
odds were, she knew, that she would not have done what
she did, that she would have become merely an append-
age of him.

And she was *not* going to sink back into being a
frightened young woman simply because he had shown
up again. Isabelle drew another deep breath, willing her
face into lines of tranquility, forcing the fear from her
eyes, firming her mouth. *There, that was better.*

Isabelle turned from the mirror and settled down to
consider her situation. She did not like the idea of being
on the same show with Michael. But there was little hope
of his leaving anytime soon, not after Danny had just
hired him—and with such obvious pride. Danny considered getting Michael away from "Eden Crossing" a tremendous coup; she could tell by the way he was crowing
about him. "Eden" was, after all, the most successful
daytime soap, whereas "All Our Tomorrows" had been
the perennial runner-up, #1 in its time slot, but #2 over-

all to "Eden." Everyone knew that that fact chafed Danny; no doubt he was hopeful that with the added attraction of Michael Traynor, their show would overtake "Eden" in the ratings. Indeed, he was probably right. Whatever Isabelle might feel about Michael Traynor, he was one of the most popular actors on daytime television, and his presence might be just the impetus they needed to push "Tomorrows" over the top.

If anyone left, if would have to be her, and Isabelle knew that she did not want to go. The show had made her very popular, and she enjoyed playing her character. Besides, the money was good, and though she could in all likelihood get a part that paid as well on another soap, she could not be absolutely sure. And with a child like Jenny, financial security was very important. Jenny would always have to have someone to look after her to some extent. That was why Isabelle kept salting away a big hunk of her salary into Jenny's trust fund every year.

Nor was it only the security of money that Jenny required. She needed to stay in the same house with the same housekeeper to pick her up from school each day, and her mother to spend regular time with her. Isabelle could not take a job on one of the soaps shooting in New York nor could she be in a movie that spent months shooting on location. Even a nighttime series required more time away from home than Isabelle wanted to spend. That was why the "Tomorrows" role was so perfect. "Tomorrows" was probably the best organized, best-run production in town; shooting was scheduled so that one's scenes were all together on certain days, with the result that even the most popular actors, such as Isabelle, worked only three or four days a week. It wasn't like other shows she had been in where she might have to be at the set all day only to shoot a scene or two. Isabelle was often able to be home with Jenny two afternoons a week after school, as well as on the weekends.

Besides, she enjoyed her role on "Tomorrows." She liked the cast and crew, and the writers and directors were good. All in all, she did not want to give up her part on it.

And there was no reason why she should, Isabelle told herself firmly. She would be acting like a schoolgirl if she left the show simply to get away from Michael Traynor. *After all, what could happen?* It wasn't as if she were in danger of being hurt by him again. No, she had learned her lesson the first time. She had gotten over him long ago, and she intended to stay that way. And she was old enough and wise enough now that he could not charm her into loving him against her better wishes.

Moreover, she doubted that he would try. Why should Michael be interested in her? She was only a girl he had had a brief fling with one summer; she obviously had not meant much to him, given how easily he had left her. If he were, by some chance, attracted to her again, all she had to do was let him know that she was not interested, and he would drop the matter. It wasn't as if he had seduced or forced her the first time; she had fallen willingly into his arms. Michael had never pushed her; she had to give him that. He could get any number of women he wanted, after all; he didn't have to pursue or push.

Surely she was adult enough to handle having to see him around the set, Isabelle told herself, even to play a scene with him now or then. It was unlikely that they would be together in many scenes. Her character, the wicked Jessica, had her hooks in Mark Townsend, the brother of the character Michael would play. And obviously, from his having auditioned with Lena, the writers intended to kindle a romance between Lena's character, Abby, and his.

It would be relatively easy to avoid him. When she did have to be around Michael, she could manage to be coolly polite. Seeing him had hit her hard this afternoon only because it was so sudden and unexpected. Once she became used to his being around, it wouldn't bother her so much. After a time, even, she might be totally unaffected.

Isabelle paused in her thoughts and smiled wryly; she wondered if any woman who was still breathing could be totally unaffected by Michael Traynor. Perhaps not, but she was armored against him better than most, she thought; she knew what could happen to her if she used poor judgment.

He wouldn't necessarily learn about Jenny. Isabelle had been careful to keep her private life separate from her job. She presumed a lot of people knew that she had a daughter, but less than a handful knew anything about that daughter. She never brought Jenny to work with her. Michael Traynor would certainly never be at her house. Even if, by some remote chance, he did see Jenny, he wouldn't necessarily assume that she was his. Isabelle could see the resemblance in her, but that wasn't to say that anyone else would. Jenny was quite small for her age; she looked more like seven or eight than ten.

The important thing, of course, was that Jenny not find out the truth. Jenny's tender feelings were easily hurt, and she could hold on to the pain for much longer than Isabelle would have thought possible. It would never do for her to know that she had a father alive and well, a father who had run out on them before he even knew about her. Worse yet would be for her to know it and see him pull away from her now. No, Jenny must not know. But that would be easy.

There was a rap on her door, and Isabelle's head came up with a snap. Her heart began to pound. For one crazy moment she thought it was Michael, coming after her to talk to her. But then Tish Klegman's voice sounded in the hall. "Miss Gray? You start shooting again in fifteen minutes."

"Oh." Isabelle pulled herself into the present with difficulty. "Yes. Of—of course. What scene?"

"Three. You and Paul and Phil, in the restaurant."

"Oh, yes." It was the scene they had been rehearsing when Danny and Carol had waltzed into practice with their new acquisition.

Isabelle glanced around her, looking for the script. All her lines seemed to have flown from her head in the last few minutes. It took her a moment to recall that she must have left the script out on the set. She sighed and closed her eyes for a moment. *She had to pull herself together. She couldn't go back out there in this frazzled condition.*

Isabelle checked her image in the mirror, straightening her clothes, tidying her hair, smoothing away a smudge of mascara beneath her eye. Callie would refresh her makeup right before they shot, of course, but she needed the confidence of looking perfect when she walked onto the soundstage. No one must suspect that Michael Traynor's arrival had upset her.

Isabelle stood up, drawing another deep breath. Then she opened the door and marched out into the hallway, head high, a faint smile on her lips as she strode along the hall and onto the soundstage.

"Isabelle," the director said, smiling. "Great. Now maybe we can get back down to business. Need to run through it again?"

Isabelle smiled, picking up her script and glancing down the page. "No, I'm fine, Lyle. Let's go ahead and shoot."

It was a long two hours later when Isabelle finally left the soundstage. She walked tiredly back to her dressing room to remove her makeup and change clothes. Despite her confident assurance to the director, she had had difficulty with the scene, blowing her lines three times in a row before she got them right. Her nerves had infected the others, with the result that the two scenes they filmed had taken them much longer than normal. She was going to have to retain control of herself better than that, Isabelle thought in disgust as she kicked off her spike heels and wriggled her toes in relief.

"Feet hurting?" a sympathetic voice said as Amanda from Wardrobe stuck her head in the door.

Isabelle cast her a wry smile. "As usual. The worst thing about playing a silver-plated bitch is the stiletto heels I have to wear. Come on in. I'll have the suit off in a sec."

Amanda came farther into the room, closing the door behind her, and picked up Isabelle's shoes from the floor. Then she took down a hanger and hung up the skirt and jacket of the elegant business suit that Isabelle had pulled off and handed to her.

"I saw the new hunk," Amanda said jokingly and fanned herself with an imaginary fan.

"Mmm," Isabelle replied noncommittally. Now she understood why Amanda personally had come to retrieve her outfit for Wardrobe. A middle-aged woman with short graying hair and no makeup, Amanda looked more like a librarian than someone in charge of glitzy costumes, but she had razor-sharp taste in clothes and loved to indulge it with the studio's money. She was equally fond of gossip and could usually be found at the center of any studio rumors.

"Word has it that you know him," she went on when Isabelle said nothing to relieve her curiosity.

"Briefly, a long time ago," Isabelle replied casually, pulling on her own jeans and a simple short-sleeved sweater. She strove to keep her tone light and uninvolved; she had to set the pattern right from the beginning. The show's gossip was the best place to start, she supposed—as long as she managed to hide all traces of residual emotion.

"We worked in the same summer theater—Shakespeare," Isabelle went on. "He was one of the professionals who had come down from New York to work with Dr. Carlysle, and I was a mere intern. I was only eighteen. I hadn't even started college yet."

She would not mention the afternoons of drinking coffee with Michael in the café across from the amphitheater or the evenings when he had walked her home, the long kisses on the porch of the big old house where the interns had roomed. She would not reveal how everything inside her had turned to Jell-O everytime Michael looked at her.

"But he remembered you. Phil said he did." Amanda gave her a conspiratorial smile. Her eyes were alight with the greedy flame of an inveterate gossip. "You must have made an impression on him."

Isabelle chuckled. "I was surprised he remembered me, truthfully. We did work together on a play, but he was

Mercutio in *Romeo and Juliet,* and I was one of the townspeople.''

She pushed out of her mind the memories of lying beneath a tree with him, the sun dappling her legs and the branches rustling over their heads, the green summer grass a tangy scent in her nostrils and the heat of Michael's body lying only inches from her as his smooth voice rolled out the lines of the play, the Shakespeare on his tongue as intoxicating as wine. There hadn't been a time, before or since, when she had felt as alive as she had that summer.

"Mercutio! I would have figured Romeo was more like it, the way he looks.'' Amanda fetched up a grandiose sigh.

"As I remember, he liked the part better. It suited him, anyway—charming and cynical.'' There had been something dark and mysterious about him. It was intriguing that his charm had a slightly rough edge, that he was not the familiar Southern boy that she'd grown up with, but a Yankee, and one with a sad history, as well. He had been orphaned at thirteen and had been bounced from foster home to foster home for a few years. His love of acting had been the thing that had saved him from following some of his New Jersey friends into a criminal life.

Isabelle had fallen for him hard. To give him credit, he had tried to ignore her, but she had been determined to reach him. She had arranged accidental meetings and flirted and schemed. It had been two weeks before he broke down and invited her out to coffee one afternoon. It had been even longer before he had finally kissed her. After that, though, they had become inseparable. Eventually, inevitably, they had come together in a cataclysmic night of lovemaking.

Three weeks later, Michael had gotten a call from his agent in New York. There had been a part in an off-Broadway play for him. He had, of course, taken it, leaving the last week of playing Mercutio to his understudy. Isabelle had been away that weekend, visiting her parents at home, and she had returned to be told by her roommate, in a tone of mock sympathy, that Michael had gone back to New York. He had left her a letter.

Isabelle would never forget the chill that invaded her being as she read that letter. He had told her of the part and said that he must leave. He loved her, the note had gone on to say, but there was no future for them. He was sure that before long she would forget all about him.

Isabelle had been too numb for tears. Those had come later, as had the saving fury, the scorn at her own naiveté. She had played the fool, she had realized; she had given her heart to a man who had wanted nothing beyond a summer fling. His career was all that mattered to him; he wanted no entanglements. All the other girls at the theater were quick to agree; they had, they assured her, seen it coming. It had happened to most of them at one time or another, they told her, and nodded their heads sagely. That was life. She had learned a valuable lesson.

Perhaps she had. But it had taken her a long, painful time to get over him. And she had always had a reminder of Michael and the pain: his daughter, Jenny.

"...but of course she always claims to have the inside scoop on everybody," Amanda was saying, giving Isabelle's suit a last straightening twitch.

Isabelle nodded vaguely and hoped she didn't need to respond. She had no idea what the woman had been saying while her own thoughts had been wandering back ten years in time.

"Well..." Amanda draped the suit over her arm and picked up the shoes from the counter where she had placed them. "See you Friday—you're not scheduled tomorrow, are you?"

"No. A day of rest tomorrow, thank heavens." Isabelle smiled at Amanda. Whatever tendencies Amanda had toward gossip, she was always on top of her job. And she had unerring taste. Isabelle was grateful to her. After all, there were those costume designers whose chief objective seemed to be to make their actresses look frumpy or sallow.

"Okay. Just wait till you see the green evening dress I've got picked out for you for the party next week. I'll show you Friday. You'll look like a million dollars in it."

"Wonderful." Isabelle summoned up enough energy for a last smile at Amanda, then sank onto her chair in front of the vanity and began to take off her heavy on-camera makeup. She combed through her heavily sprayed and arranged hair until it was back into its normal loose style over her shoulders.

Free of the makeup and elaborate hairdo, she felt better. She rolled her head from side to side, letting the tension of the day begin to drain from her. She thought about the fact that in a few minutes she would be home with Jenny—and there would be a whole day alone tomorrow to marshal her inner strength before she had to see Michael Traynor again.

Isabelle slipped her feet into her ragged sneakers and grabbed her bag, heading out the door. She walked down the hall, nodding at the people she passed, and out the front door. The sun struck her like a blow, and she hurriedly dug in her bag for her sunglasses. She didn't notice the knot of people standing on the sidewalk in front of the building until it was too late.

Michael Traynor was chatting with two of the writers. Isabelle's stomach clenched. She hadn't been prepared to see him again. But she summoned up a smile and walked past them with a breezy wave and a "hi," continuing toward her car in the parking lot without breaking stride.

"Isabelle! Wait!" She glanced back and saw with an inward groan that Michael had peeled away from the others and was walking toward her.

Two

Isabelle hesitated. The nerves in her stomach were jumping. She didn't have the strength to deal with Michael right now. She would have liked to turn and continue walking to her car. But her pride would not let her. She did not want Michael to think that he was able to affect her in any way. So she squared her shoulders and waited, putting a faintly questioning and impatient expression on her face.

"I'm sorry," she said, smiling impersonally. "I was just about to leave."

Michael stopped in front of her. Isabelle was disconcertingly aware of his body, his charisma, the magnetism of his blue eyes. She fought a sudden surge of sensual memories—the warmth and strength of his arms around her, the delicious taste of his mouth, the shivers of delight his hands had roused on her body.

"I've been hanging around waiting for you," Michael began. "We need to talk."

Isabelle raised her eyebrows coolly, though inside, her nerves were jangling. "We do?"

"Yes." Michael frowned. "We're going to be working together. I—It would be easier if things were straight between us."

"As far as I know, there isn't anything 'between us,'" Isabelle answered, pleased at the indifference she had managed to inject into her voice. It was difficult, considering the way Michael's cobalt-blue eyes were boring into her.

"There was once," Michael replied seriously. "I don't want that to be a problem."

"No problem," Isabelle returned lightly. "I hadn't even thought of you in years until Danny brought you in today."

"I could see that it was a surprise. I had assumed that they'd told you we were negotiating. I'm sorry, I didn't want it to be a shock to you."

"Michael…" Isabelle made her voice crisp, using every acting skill she possessed to sound faintly amused. "I'm afraid you don't have the power to shock me anymore."

His eyebrows rose lazily. "Ah…a direct hit." He shrugged. "Well, I'm glad to hear that you're okay with my joining the cast. I want to work with you without either one of us being submarined by a lot of things from the past."

"I'm not a teenager anymore, Michael. I don't fall in and out of love at the drop of a hat. And I used up my supply of tears where you were concerned years ago. If it will relieve your mind, then I'm happy to tell you that my crush on you is most assuredly a thing of the past. I doubt very seriously that you and I will be working together much, but when we do, I'm sure that it will be no problem for us to maintain a professional attitude."

Isabelle cringed inside at how prissy she sounded. No doubt he would think she had turned into some kind of wooden prig. *Well, what did it matter what he thought of her?*

Amusement flashed through his eyes for a moment, lightening them, but then it was gone, and he merely nodded. "Good. I'm glad to hear that. I—uh, guess I'll see you around."

Isabelle wanted to childishly retort, "Not if I see you first," but she refrained. Instead, she nodded briefly at Michael and turned and strode off to her car. She resisted the impulse to look back and see if he was watching her. By the time she reached her car and could turn in his direction without it seeming purposeful, she saw that he had left. She sank into the driver's seat, the adrenaline that had come to her rescue earlier now oozing out of her system and leaving her more drained than before. She leaned her forehead wearily against the steering wheel.

God, she hoped all the days weren't going to be like this.

Jenny was riding her bike in front of the house when Isabelle turned into their driveway. With her little spaniel puppy sitting in the basket behind her seat, Jenny was intently pedaling the three-wheel cycle around and around the drive in front of the garage. It was a large cycle, with a front wheel and frame like a bicycle, but with two wide-spaced bicycle wheels across the back to give it stability. When Jenny had outgrown her tricycle, she had wanted to graduate to a bike, but she still had some difficulties with her balance, making a bicycle too dangerous. Isabelle had seen an old lady with a plastic sack of aluminum cans wheeling along a street in Hollywood on a contraption like this one day, and she had realized that it would be perfect for Jenny.

"Mommy!" Jenny cried when she saw Isabelle, and waved enthusiastically. Her eyes lit up in the way that indicated excitement and pleasure, though her mouth and face retained its usual serious expression. Jenny was not much given to smiling.

Isabelle's daughter was small and pale. Her hair was thick and black, cut short in a practical bob. Thick dark eyebrows cut startlingly across her face, and it was this that gave her the most resemblance to Michael—that and the penetrating blue of her eyes. She wore big round red-rimmed glasses that emphasized the pixieish shape of her face.

"Hi, sweetheart." Isabelle parked in the garage, then got out of the car and walked over to her. "How's my girl?"

"I'm fine. I'm giving Patience a ride."

"I see. That's nice of you."

Patience, their dainty liver-and-white Cavalier spaniel, leapt lightly out of her basket and trotted over to Isabelle, wagging her tail. Isabelle bent to pet her. Patience was an extremely sweet-tempered dog who submitted herself resignedly to Jenny's play and did nothing but walk away if Jenny unintentionally squeezed a leg or pulled an ear. Isabelle had bought her and named her for precisely that quality. Prudence, on the other hand, their large smoky gray Persian cat, made it a point to stay well out of Jenny's way and always kept a wary eye on her unless Isabelle was with them.

"Hello, Patience," Isabelle murmured, giving her an extra few rubs to reward her good nature.

Jenny cautiously disembarked from her vehicle and hurried over to her mother, holding her arms wide for a hug. Isabelle pulled her close and squeezed her. Whatever else she felt for Michael Traynor, she could not help but be grateful to him for giving her this girl.

She had not always felt that way, of course. She had cried herself to sleep night after night when she realized that she was pregnant, almost two months after Michael left her. He had tried once or twice to call her during the summer, but she had stubbornly refused to talk to him. When she discovered she was pregnant, she had fallen into despair and she had considered finally talking to him. But he didn't call her again, and she would not take the step of calling him.

Instead, she had sleepwalked her way through the first semester of her freshman year, then returned home at Christmas and broke the news to her parents. Predictably, her well-to-do Southern parents had been genteelly horrified at the news. When she told them that she intended to keep the baby and raise it, her father had argued with her incessantly. He wanted her to have an abortion; he told her over and over how it would ruin her life and be a perpetual burden to her.

To Isabelle's surprise, it had been her mother, always the picture of frail, proper Southern femininity, who had finally said, "Oh, Harrington, hush. Of course she's not going to get rid of her baby. Whatever are you thinking of? We'll just have to make adjustments, that's all."

The adjustments had been far worse than any of them had expected, however. Jenny had been born with a heart defect, pinched-faced and bluish. For weeks, it had been a daily struggle for her to stay alive. She underwent three surgeries in the first two years of her life and another one when she was six to repair her heart. All her life she had remained small and been slow to develop, and she had been hit hard by any childhood virus or infection. Since the final operation, she had been able to lead a fairly normal life physically, to play and even ride her bike without gasping for breath or having to stop frequently.

However, nothing could repair the damage that had been done to Jenny's brain in the first few weeks of her life when her weak heart had not pumped enough oxygen-rich blood to her brain. She had been slow to develop both mentally and physically, walking later, talking later and never completely achieving the skills of other children her age.

The first few years of Jenny's life, she had occupied all Isabelle's time. College, her plans to act, everything had fallen by the wayside as she had struggled to keep Jenny alive and well. Once again, it had been Isabelle's mother who had pulled her aside and pointed out that Isabelle could not sacrifice herself for her daughter, that she had to create some kind of life for herself, as well.

Isabelle had been scared, but she had known that her mother was right. She had started in a small way by going back to college, but she had quickly realized that she was light-years away from the carefree freshmen in her classes. Finally, she had decided to move to Los Angeles and try to make it in the career she had always wanted: acting. If she could not make it, there would be time enough later to come back and build another, safer career for herself.

It had been tough, and Isabelle knew that it would probably have been impossible without the extra money her parents had provided for Jenny's welfare. Isabelle had had no life outside of her work and her daughter. She went to auditions; she took acting lessons; she worked part-time jobs. The rest of the time she spent with Jenny.

There had been no time for men and, frankly, Isabelle had had little interest in them. She had gotten a few jobs in commercials and walk-ons in two nighttime series. Then her first real break had come: she had been hired as a daily on one of the soap operas. The response to her had been so good that her two weeks had expanded into two months and finally into a year's contract. Then, almost three years ago, she had moved to "Tomorrows" and her current role as Jessica Connors O'Neal Randall, the town villainess.

She had become enormously popular in the role. She had the perfect looks for the part of the local siren: thick, long black hair, vivid emerald-green eyes and a voluptuous figure. But it was her acting skills that had brought her such a devoted following. She was able to make her character not only wicked, but was able also to invest her with a sense of humor and even a hint of vulnerability that had made it possible for viewers to love her even as they hated her. Last year, when the writers had put Jessica in a life-threatening car crash in which she had lost the child she was carrying, viewers had written in, frantic at the thought that Jessica was going to die.

Because of her popularity in the role, Isabelle was now financially secure. She had been able to buy a lovely secluded house with plenty of yard for Jenny to play in. She could send Jenny to an excellent school and pay for a housekeeper/companion for her daughter. She had even been able to pay back her parents for the money they'd lent her during her first years in L.A. But money was the only thing that had changed for them. Isabelle still had only one interest outside of work, and that was her daughter.

She squeezed Jenny tightly to her now. "How was school?"

"Fine. I made something."

"You did? How nice. May I see it?"

Jenny shook her head. "I'm not supposed to tell you."

"I see. A special present, then."

Jenny nodded. "We made it this morning. But I can't tell you."

"That's all right. I'll see it when you bring it home."

Jenny nodded. "Miss Bright said, 'Shh.'" She brought her forefinger up to her lips and made an exaggerated gesture of silence. "I don't like it, they say. 'Don't talk.'"

"Who says, Jenny? Miss Albright?"

Jenny nodded emphatically. "Miss Bright says 'Don't talk,' and I only asked... He was drawing, see, like this." She made big circular motions with her right hand, as if drawing in air. "And he—" She pulled her hands apart as if ripping something.

"He tore up his paper?" Isabelle wasn't sure exactly what Jenny was talking about; she sometimes had trouble following her disjointed, repetitive way of speaking even after years of experience.

Jenny's dark head came down in the same hard nod. She was clearly feeling indignant. "Yes! And Miss Bright, she said, 'Don't talk.' I don't like that."

"I'm sure not. You just wanted to see what he was drawing, right?"

"'Whatcha doing?'" Jenny agreed. "'Whatcha doing?'"

Isabelle repressed a smile. This was Jenny's favorite question of any- and everyone. No doubt some other child in her class had resented her asking it.

"Well, I'm sure Miss Albright didn't want you disturbing the other students. Apparently he didn't like it when you asked him to let you see."

"He's a poophead," Jenny commented. Then she added, "Kevin said 'He's a poophead.'"

"I bet Miss Albright didn't like that."

"Uh-uh." Jenny shook her head exaggeratedly. "She said, 'No, no, no.'"

"And what have you been doing since you came home from school?" Isabelle asked, deciding it was probably better to switch off this subject. Miss Albright would probably not appreciate Jenny's implanting the forbidden word in her mind with further repetitions.

"I gave Patience a ride." Jenny leaned down and patted the dog firmly on the head.

"Good. But don't ride her around too much, or she might get sick."

"She likes to ride. Lady didn't like to ride."

"No. Lady was getting a little old for riding." Lady had been their first dog, a rather cantankerous old miniature poodle that had been Isabelle's mother's dog. Jenny had cried so much at leaving her when they moved to Los Angeles that Frances had given her to them.

"Lady's gone now. Lady's in Heaven," Jenny pointed out.

"I know. And I'm sure she's very happy."

"Lady's in Heaven now. We took her—she went—weeks ago."

"Even longer than that."

"She went to the dog hospital. Now she's in Heaven."

"That's right. Why don't you put up your bicycle and let's go inside and see what Irma has fixed for supper?" Isabelle suggested.

"Hot dog and chips."

"That's what we're having for supper?" Isabelle smiled. "I imagine Irma's cooked something healthier than that."

"*I* had it. Hot dog and chips. That's what I wanted."

"When you came home from school? That's what Irma gave you for a snack after school?"

Jenny nodded and started over to her cycle, saying again, "Hot dog and chips."

She walked her big tricycle into the garage and carefully stowed it away in its place beside Isabelle's car. Isabelle waited for her, and they walked in the back door. Irma Pena, their housekeeper, turned and grinned at them, whisking off her apron.

"Ah, Mrs. Gray. I'm glad you're home. I'm sorry, but I have to run tonight." Usually Irma was happy to stay longer with Jenny when Isabelle ran late in the evenings. "I have to pick Estrellita up at school. They're practicing a play, and I have to be there at eight-thirty."

"I'm sorry I kept you late. We ran over at the studio today."

"*Sí*. No problem." Irma waved away Isabelle's explanation and apology. "I got plenty of time still. But I don't like for Estrellita to have to stand around and wait, you know—you never know what can happen." She shook her head, clicking her tongue, as she crossed the room and picked up her handbag and keys from the counter. "Terrible thing, when a girl isn't safe at school."

"Yes, it is."

Jenny was frowning, listening to her. "I'm safe," she said.

"Of course you are, precious one." Irma smiled at her. "I was talking about something else. Don't you worry about it."

"Don't talk to strangers," Jenny told her solemnly. "Then you're safe."

"That's right. Never talk to strangers," Isabelle agreed, waving to Irma as she bustled out the door.

"I never do. Miss Bright told us. Strangers might—might—"

"They might hurt you," Isabelle supplied gently. "That's why Miss Albright told you not to talk to them."

This was a lesson that Jenny had been taught regularly for years, both in school and out. She repeated the words often, proud that she had learned the lesson, but for all her words about it, Isabelle was not at all sure that Jenny would heed the advice. She was impulsive and affectionate, prone to hug everyone she met, and Isabelle could easily imagine her wandering off with anyone, hand in hand, while she faithfully repeated her maxim of "Don't talk to strangers." For that reason, she made sure that Irma was always there to pick Jenny up as soon as school was let out, and she never let Jenny play outside their fenced-in yard.

Irma had left grilled tuna and a broccoli-and-rice casserole on the stove for them, and Isabelle dished them up and carried them to the table while Jenny painstakingly set the table. Jenny continued to chatter all through dinner and afterward, until finally Isabelle told her that it was time for a quiet period and sent her off to her room to play by herself for a few minutes.

Isabelle kicked off her shoes and stretched out on the couch. Her head was pounding and had been for some time, she realized. Prudence uncoiled her large, smoky gray body from the mantel where she liked to perch and leapt lightly down. She came over to the couch and rubbed herself against it beneath Isabelle's head, emitting plaintive meows.

"Hey, kitty," Isabelle murmured, stroking her hand down the cat's back. "You're looking as fat and sassy as ever."

She closed her eyes, still stroking the cat, reveling in the peace of the moment. She needed it, after a day like this one had been.

Taking this time to herself—turning off Jenny's incessant chatter and separating herself from the child for a few moments—had been one of the hardest things for Isabelle to learn to do. She had been accustomed since Jenny's birth to spending all her time caring for her and worrying about her. She felt guilty for spending time away from Jenny when she worked even though Jenny was going to a special school that did wonders for her. When she was at home, she felt it was imperative that she give Jenny her constant undivided attention. There were times when Jenny's disjointed, repetitive chattering scraped her nerves raw, but she gritted her teeth and listened and responded.

It had been Jenny's teacher, at a parent's night, that had taken her aside and advised her to tell Jenny when she had talked enough, when Isabelle needed to be by herself or enjoy a few minutes of quiet.

Isabelle had felt—and looked—a trifle shocked. "But I want her to feel that what she says is important to me. I think I should listen to her."

"Of course you should. But not all the time. I've been watching you tonight, and you're letting Jenny dominate every moment of your time. That isn't good for her, Ms. Gray. She needs, just like every other child, to know her limits. She needs structure. You aren't doing her any favors. It's pity, not love. Just think about it. If Jenny were a 'normal' child, would you allow her to rattle on all the time? I don't think so. You would teach her manners. You'd know that she needs to learn to let others talk, that she's not the only person in the world. Jenny needs to learn that, too."

Isabelle had stared at her, much struck by her words. Then she had thanked her, and ever since that day she had made it a point to now and then stop Jenny's prattling and to take a few minutes out of her evening to be completely alone.

Prudence jumped up onto the couch and settled onto Isabelle's stomach, letting out her low, throaty purr. The sound was hypnotic, soothing, and Isabelle felt the knots of tension gradually seeping out of her muscles. She was just drifting into sleep when Jenny came back into the room, dragging one of her dolls by the hair.

"Hi," she said, plopping down on the couch at Isabelle's feet. "Whatcha doing?"

Isabelle smiled. Ten or fifteen minutes was usually Jenny's limit for leaving one alone. "Nothing. Just being lazy."

She sat up and cuddled Jenny to her side. "Well, what do you say we watch a little TV together? Would you like that?"

"Sure."

Isabelle picked up the remote control and flicked the television on. Jenny was immediately absorbed, staring at the screen, lips slightly parted. Isabelle bent and kissed the top of her head.

She would get past this Michael Traynor thing with all the ease and grace she could muster, Isabelle promised herself. Nothing, absolutely nothing, was going to be allowed to interfere with the tranquil life she and Jenny had created for themselves.

Michael Traynor walked over to the window of his hotel room and looked out. The swimming pool lay below amidst short palm trees, emerald-green grass and light-edged walkways. It was a landscaping work of art, but Michael didn't even notice the view. Instead, he stared rather blankly off into the distance; his mind was on Isabelle.

He had known she was on "Tomorrows." Truthfully—though he would not have told her that—it was one of the things that had intrigued him when his agent told him Danny Archer wanted him for the show. He had been restless, tired of "Eden Crossing," the show on which he had been for almost four years, tired even of New York City and the opportunity of doing live theater. The money Archer offered had been a good deal better, and L.A. offered more opportunity for other acting jobs, as well as a change of scenery. Besides, the thought of Isabelle teased at his mind. *What was she like now? How would he feel when he saw her?*

The memories of their long-ago love had stirred within him. He could not remember ever feeling such passion before or since. It had torn out his heart to leave her. The fact that he was sure he was doing the right thing, the noble thing, hadn't made the pain any less. There had been many times when he had given in and phoned her, ready to beg her to come to New York and be with him, but, fortunately, he supposed, she had refused to even speak with him.

Michael sighed. *Apparently Isabelle still despised him just as much.* He thought about the moment when he had first seen Isabelle today, standing there on the soundstage with the others. He had known that he would see her, but the actuality of her stunned him. She was beautiful. Over the years he had come to believe that he had exaggerated her beauty, but now he knew that he had not. If anything, she was even more lovely than he had remembered. Time and experience, he realized as he came closer to her, had given her perfect features a character that they had lacked when she was eighteen. His palms had started to sweat and his heart had begun to pound when Danny Archer guided him across the floor to meet her.

He turned away from the window and flopped down on his bed, linking his hands behind his head. He closed his eyes, remembering the first time he had ever seen Isabelle. Then she had been standing on the stage in Virginia, helping set up a flat of painted scenery for the background. Her black hair had tumbled down her back, and her jean shorts and cropped T-shirt had done little to hide her curvaceous figure. He had known as soon as he saw her that she was trouble: far too gorgeous and far too young. He had been right. She had been only eighteen, and she had the kind of beauty that haunted men. Within a month he was desperately in love with her.

A faint smile touched Michael's lips as he thought about lying stretched out on his bed in his room with her that summer, naked arms and legs entwined, their perspiration mingling as they kissed and caressed and moaned. He could still remember the thrum of the ancient air-conditioning unit that barely cooled the air as their bodies moved together. He could remember the taste of her skin, warm and damp, smelling sweetly of perfume, the delicious weight of her breasts in his hands, the utter glory of being buried deep within her.

Michael groaned softly and rolled onto his side. Just recalling the moments of making love with her had been enough to arouse him. He wondered if it would still be as heavenly to go to bed with her.

Not that he was likely to get a chance, he reminded himself wryly. Isabelle obviously wished to have nothing to do with him. This morning when Danny introduced him, Isabelle had looked straight through him, her face as cold and remote as an iceberg, and greeted him as if he had been someone she had once barely known. Afterward, in the parking lot, she had told him so straight out, just in case he hadn't gotten the message. *Their love affair had been a long time ago, and she hadn't even thought of him in years.*

Michael grimaced. He didn't know what he had expected. *A woman doesn't greet you with cries of pleasure when you've left them in the past, even if it was with the best of motives. And after ten years, well, it wasn't very likely that she'd have any feeling about him one way or another.* He wasn't even sure how he had hoped she might react. He wouldn't have wanted her to have missed and mourned him all these years; after all, one of the main reasons he'd left had been because he knew she was too young to really be sure she was in love. He'd wanted her to be able to grow up, to go to college, to meet a man and fall in love for real, forever, not be stuck with an eighteen-year-old's infatuation. No, he hadn't hoped that Isabelle would be sad or holding a grudge.

But he had hoped that she would not dismiss him so coolly or quickly. He had thought that perhaps she would feel the same tingles of excitement he had at seeing her again. There had lurked in him some faint, strange, unreasonable idea that when they saw each other again, sparks would be struck again. That fate might have brought them together to give them another chance.

Michael shrugged and stood up. He was, after all, too old to believe in fate or second chances. He had a job, and it started tomorrow. He better get ready for that. As for Isabelle Gray...well, she wanted to keep him at arm's length, and that was exactly what he would do. They might work together, but that was all. He'd take care to avoid her the rest of the time.

Still, he couldn't help but remember her kiss....

Three

Isabelle took the script Tish handed her and quickly perused it to get a sense of her scenes the following week. All around her in the lounge, other actors and actresses were doing the same thing. She sneaked a glance at Ben Ivor. He was running his forefinger down the pages, counting under his breath. She cut her eyes toward Felice McIntyre, sitting beside her. Felice, who played the sweet, perennially martyred Townsend sister, Christine, on the show, put her hand up to stifle a giggle. Ben Ivor's obsession with the number of lines he was given per week was a running joke between them. He played one of the minor regular characters on the show, the resident bartender who also got up now and then to sing on the nightclub's small stage.

"Fourteen lines!" Ivor exclaimed in disgust. "I can't believe it. I thought last week was bad enough, but fourteen!'' He jumped up, slamming the script shut and started out the door. ''I'm going to talk to Karen.''

He stalked out of the lounge to find the head writer of the show. Felice pulled a cigarette out of the pack on the table before her and lit it languidly. ''If Karen's smart, she'll have left the building already.''

Isabelle chuckled. ''I heard that last week she was forced to resort to hiding in the women's rest room to escape him.''

''I heard. Poor Ben. Since they wrote Selman out, he hasn't had anyone to compare lines with. He has nothing else to do except harass Karen.''

Felice flipped through the pages. ''Oh, God, they're going on with this hypnosis thing. I can't imagine what else Christine could possibly dredge up from her past. She's had every illness and tragedy known to man.''

''There's incest,'' Isabelle pointed out. ''They've never dropped that on her.''

''Incest? In the saintly Townsend clan? Get real. Besides, they just did the incest thing with Lena last year.''

''That's right. I'd forgotten. Oh, well, that's never stopped them yet.'' Isabelle thumbed through her pages. ''Hey, you and I get into a cat fight on Wednesday.''

''Really?'' Felice looked delighted. ''What page? Is there any physical stuff? I always like a real knock-down drag-out.''

''Mmm. I slap you, and you turn a bowl of soup over my head.'' She made a face. ''Great. Why is it that I'm always the one who gets drinks thrown in her face or food dumped in her lap?''

''Because you always have to get your comeuppance in some form, my dear. After all, Jessica always manages to slither out of the consequences for the nasty things she does.''

Isabelle continued flipping through the script while Felice perused the fight scene. When Isabelle reached the following Friday's filming, she froze. Both hers and Michael's names jumped off the page at her. She began to read, and with each line she grew stiffer and tauter.

"No! I can't." She looked up and glanced around the room, even though she knew it was useless to seek out one of the writers there on the day they handed out the scripts. They were usually out of the building, leaving the head writer to deal with the actors' complaints.

"What is it?" Felice glanced up at her, startled by the note of real panic in Isabelle's voice. "What have they got down for you?"

"They have me trying to seduce Curtis Townsend."

"Michael Traynor?" Felice grinned. "What are you complaining about? Most of the actresses on this show are panting for a chance to do a love scene with him. I'm just sorry I play his sister. I heard Sally was in Carol's office the other day trying to persuade her that her character was a much better one to pair Michael with than Lena's. Of course, he and Lena haven't exactly lit up the screen. I hear Danny is really disappointed with the lack of interest the viewers are showing in their couple. They get tons of letters about Michael, but most of them think he and Lena together are a yawn. That's probably why they're trying to spice it up by having you seduce him."

Isabelle hardly heard Felice. All she could think of was the scene on the paper before her. *She simply could not do it!*

Naively, she realized now, she had been congratulating herself on how well she had handled Michael's presence on the show. Most of the time she had avoided the snack area and lounge, the place where she was most likely to run into him. If she did happen to find herself in

the same room with him, she had made sure that she
stayed on the opposite side of it. When she met him in the
halls, she gave him a nod or a terse hello in greeting.
Fortunately, he had not attempted to talk to her again,
other than their stiff, formal greetings. She had, finally,
grown accustomed to seeing him, so that it was not the
same shock to her nervous system whenever she came
upon him unexpectedly.

Their first scene together had come two weeks after he
arrived, and Isabelle had been stiff and nervous, mentally braced to ward off his charm. After they shot it, she
had almost cried in her dressing room, sure that it had
been the worst performance she'd ever given. But when
she'd looked at it later, she had seen that it hadn't been
bad. The edginess and faint atmosphere of hostility had
worked well. Michael's character was, fortunately, written as her enemy; he was about the only male in the fic-
tional town of Lansfield who saw through her beauty to
the wicked character beneath. They had had a few scenes
together since then, and Isabelle had found it easy to
portray the antagonism between them. She was beginning to believe that everything would work out all right.
She could handle the intermittent, hostile scenes with
Michael, and the rest of the time she could avoid him.

But now this....

Isabelle stood up abruptly. "I have to talk to Karen."

Felice gaped at her. "Are you serious?"

"Of course I am. I don't want to do this. It—it isn't
right." She glanced down at her friend and, seeing her
astonished expression, added hastily, "For the part, I
mean. They're enemies. There's no way Jessica would
make a play for him."

Felice shrugged and said wryly, "Then he'd be the only
one in town."

Isabelle grimaced. "Well, she's a slut, of course, but she isn't *stupid*." She turned and started for the door.

Just at that moment, Michael Traynor, sitting across the room, raised his head and turned to look at her. His face was impassive, but when his eyes met hers, Isabelle knew that he had been reading the same pages she had. His dark eyebrows, distinctively straight, quirked up into a humorous inverted V, and a faint smile touched his lips.

Isabelle's stomach lurched, as if she'd taken a sudden step down. She could feel a blush spreading up her face and it infuriated her, which only made her blush worse. She pressed her lips together and jerked her eyes away from his. Keeping her face straight ahead, she strode from the room and out into the hall.

Karen's office was on the floor above. Her secretary gave Isabelle a fleeting glance and pushed the intercom button, announcing her in a bored voice. A moment later Karen opened the door to her office.

"Isabelle!" She looked puzzled. "I'm surprised to see you. Come in, come in."

She ushered Isabelle in with good humor. Isabelle had rarely come to her to argue any point about the scripts; she was an easy actress to work with, and it wasn't difficult to be pleasant to her.

"Don't tell me you're unhappy with your script," she commented as she went back around to sit behind her desk. "We've given you two crackerjack scenes next week."

"I know. I'm sure they're wonderful." Isabelle sat down stiffly. Now that she was here, she wasn't sure what to say. They *were* good scenes. Most of the actresses on the show would be delighted to have two such prominent scenes in one week. *How was she to explain that she sim-*

ply could not play a seduction scene with Michael Traynor?

"Then what's the problem?" Karen frowned.

"There isn't one with the fight with Felice. It's very funny and vicious and full of great lines."

Karen smiled, pleased. "Judy Weinburg wrote it. I'm really pleased with her work. I'm giving her more and more of Jessica's scripts."

"That's great. She writes very well." Isabelle forced a smile. "It's the seduction scene that worries me. I—well, it doesn't ring true to me. Why would Jessica try to seduce Curtis? They thoroughly dislike each other. She knows what he thinks of her and that he's undermining her influence with Mark."

"It doesn't have anything to do with her being *attracted* to him. She's trying to find some way to control him, like she does with everyone. Why, it's the most natural thing in the world for her to do. He hasn't fallen under her spell like all the other men, so she's decided to bring out the heavy guns. It's the way she gains power over men. Curtis is a real eye-opener for Jessica, the first man who has been able to resist her charms. I think we're going to have a lot of fun with that."

"But—" Isabelle thought frantically "—but why would she risk doing that with Mark's brother? I mean, Mark has been taking her side when Curtis tries to make him see what she's like. She has a good hold on Mark and his money, and she wants it to stay that way. She wouldn't risk Curtis telling his brother what she had done. And you know Goody-Two-Shoes Curtis would run right over and tell Mark."

"Nah. He's too noble. He couldn't bear to hurt his brother that way. He'll turn her down and despise her all the more for it, but he'll keep his mouth shut. And Jessica is desperate enough to risk it because Curtis is convincing Mark to go work at that medical mission in Central America. She's afraid she'll lose him.''

''I know—what is all that stuff about this medical mission? Where did that come from?''

''Jim Ehrlich's taking a leave from the show in a few weeks, so we have to find some reason for Mark to disappear for a month. We figured he should do something noble like go work in a medical mission in Central America. Then we can tie it in with the drug-smuggling story, and the timing'll be perfect for May sweeps.''

''Oh. I see. I didn't know Jim was leaving. But why do this scene with Curtis? I mean, he and Jessica don't have any real story together. They just sort of touch peripherally because of Mark.''

''*Right now* they don't,'' Karen said significantly, and her words sent a chill through Isabelle. ''But we've got to do something with Jessica while Mark's gone. I figure sparring with Curtis would be a good way to fill some of her time. We've been getting good viewer response on you and Michael.''

''What?'' Isabelle looked at her blankly. ''But we've only been in a few scenes together.''

''Yeah, but the chemistry's good. Viewers like a good feud almost as much as a good love story—maybe better. Whenever you and Michael are on screen together, the sparks fly. We've had a lot of fan mail saying they'd like to see more of Jessica and Curtis. Lena and Michael's relationship isn't progressing the way we'd planned. We may have to take them along slowly, give the fans more time to build an interest in them, and in the meantime we'll play up the hostility between Curtis and Jessica.''

"So—" Isabelle had to stop and clear her throat before she could continue. She felt as if her vocal cords had tightened into rigidity. "You mean that Michael and I will be having more scenes together?"

"Yeah. We're going to change the story line some. People love Michael—they think he's a hunk. So we have to be careful to keep them watching him. We can't let them get bored with his romantic story." She paused, then hastened to assure Isabelle. "It'll be great for you, too. Otherwise, you're hanging in limbo while Mark's out, with nothing to work on but that old resentment of Christine, and that's getting kind of tired."

That was true, Isabelle knew. People would get a kick out of this fight between them next week, but their conflict was from the past, and people would soon grow bored with it. The worst thing about all this was that Karen was right. A running feud with Curtis over his brother would spark up her story as much as Michael's. She knew how damaging it could be to one's popularity when one's love interest left a show. There had been one actor who was quite popular on "Tomorrows" whose storyline had died because his wife had been killed off. He had drifted around being sad and having people commiserate with him for a few weeks, but his scenes had grown fewer and fewer, and fan mail for him had tailed off. Finally he had been written out, too.

Isabelle sighed. "I know. You're right."

Karen gave her a puzzled look. "Then why so downcast? What's the problem?"

How could she tell Karen that the thought of doing any kind of love scene, even a rejected seduction, with Michael Traynor scared her right down to her toes? Isabelle thought of kissing Michael, and her stomach turned to ice. She could remember vividly the way his lips had felt on hers, the feverish shivers that had run through her every time he kissed her. *What if she still reacted that way? It would be so humiliating!*

Worse than that, it might stir up old feelings, feelings whose size and intensity frightened Isabelle. She had promised herself long ago that she would never again be so vulnerable to a man as she had been to Michael Traynor. It frightened her to think that if she kissed him, even in pretense for the show, she might once again feel as she had when she had been a girl of eighteen. That she might open up even the tiniest crack in her emotional armor.

But it wouldn't do to let the head writer know that she was allowing her personal feelings to interfere with her role on the show. "Nothing, really. I guess I get tired of Jessica trying to solve all her problems by sleeping with some guy."

"But that's what people love about Jessica!" Karen responded brightly, chuckling. "She can always be counted on to inject some sex into the hour."

What Karen didn't know was that sex was the last thing Isabelle wanted injected into her nonrelationship with Michael.

"Thanks for talking to me about it." Isabelle forced a faint smile and stood up. There was nothing else she could do to stave it off. More strenuous objections to the scene with no more reason than she had would appear strange to the writers and the producers and would probably stir up the kind of gossip she always strove to avoid. All she could do now was prepare herself— strengthen her defenses for the scene next Friday.

"There!" The hairdresser stepped back, opening her hands in an expansive gesture, and beamed at the reflection in the mirror.

Isabelle looked into the mirror. Debbie had done an even better job than usual. Her hair was a sexy tangle of gleaming curls. Combined with the low-cut, clinging black cocktail dress she wore, it created the perfect image of a beautiful, wild female predator on the prowl.

Isabelle's hands felt cold as ice. She did not want to do this. But she said only, "You've outdone yourself this time, Debbie."

"Well, you know, your first big scene with Michael..." She grinned conspiratorially.

Isabelle thought sourly that Michael had obviously wrapped the hairstylist around his finger. *Of course, the same could be said for most of the women involved in the soap opera.* Sometimes Isabelle felt like revealing to them what a heartless, self-absorbed bastard he was—but, of course, she would never open up her personal life to such intimate inspection.

She stood and smoothed down the tight-fitting short skirt. She had to admit that Amanda had done a great job of finding just the right dress, too—devastatingly sexy without crossing over the borderline to sluttish. It was perfectly suited to her figure and also revealed a tempting amount of her long legs.

Isabelle clutched her script, as she had all during the time she had been in Makeup and Hairstyling. The slim blue-bound book was now permanently curled up from being twisted in her hands. She set off down the hallway to the soundstage, trying to look both nonchalant and businesslike—and not at all as if her knees were quaking.

She had worked all week to prepare herself for today's shooting, but now that it had arrived, she found herself feeling as anxious as she had when she first learned about it. She was flushed and overheated one moment and the next, freezing. Her mouth was dry as cotton. At the moment she could not remember a single one of her lines. All she could think about was the fact that she was going to kiss Michael, that she was going to have to radiate sexual invitation toward him, to lure and seduce him and put herself right back in the danger of his arms.

Rationally she knew that nothing was going to happen. It was, after all, a scene for TV, and it would be shot in front of a director and crew. It wouldn't be real, and she had shot many such scenes before without a qualm. There would be no emotion in their kiss; it would be faked. Besides, there was no danger of her feelings for Michael returning. She had gotten over him years ago; there was no feeling toward him left inside her except antipathy. She was much too mature now to be conquered by a sexy kiss—not that he would even try to make it sexy. Surely Michael had no more interest than she in trying to rekindle the fire that had once burned between them.

But all the reasonable arguments in the world couldn't stand up against the ice in the pit of her stomach.

She walked onto the soundstage, where the crew was bustling around making adjustments to lights and cameras. Isabelle carefully picked her way over the snaking obstacles of thick cables and cords. The set was the living room of Jessica's condo. On the set next to it, the elegant living room of the Townsend house. They had just finished shooting a large party scene, and a few of the actors were still strolling away from it.

Paul, who played the lawyer ex-husband of Christine Townsend, Chase Manning, caught sight of Isabelle, and his eyebrows vaulted up exaggeratedly.

"My, my, my, don't you look yummy," Paul said. "You know, Izzy, sometimes I get so used to seeing you every day I forget how incredible-looking you really are."

To her chagrin, Isabelle felt a blush creeping up her neck into her face. She rolled her eyes. "It's the hairstyle and the dress."

"Yeah, right." Vivian laughed. "I wish I had that hairstyle and dress."

Isabelle couldn't help turning her eyes toward the condo set, where Michael sat, waiting, his script in his hand as if he'd been going over his lines one last time. But he was not looking at the script. He was looking straight at Isabelle. His eyes flickered down her body for a fraction of a second, then returned. She lifted her chin and walked, stony-faced, to the set.

"Isabelle," Lyle Gordon, the director, said in greeting and came over to join them. "You look great." His eyes skimmed over her in a professional, asexual way. "Perfect. Okay, let's block and run through it quickly. It's a pretty simple scene—just you two."

Isabelle nodded, trying to keep her attention on him. Her gaze kept wandering traitorously toward Michael, and her nerves were jumping like live wires. She had to get herself under control. She could not let Michael see how nervous doing this scene with him made her. She concentrated on pulling herself into her character. It was difficult to do today; all her acting skills seemed suddenly to have deserted her.

"Okay," Lyle went on. "Now, Jessica is furious because Mark has decided to go work in the medical mission in San Pedro. She's sure it's all Curtis's fault. But, of course, being Jessica, she hides that anger and is going to try to get even with Curtis, as well as cancel his influence with Mark. So, Isabelle, remember to let some of the anger peek through now and then."

"I will." Anger, she thought, would not be the hard part.

They walked through the scene, blocking it, setting marks for the camera angles. Then they ran through it once, rehearsing it. Isabelle was edgy and stiff. Even though rehearsal didn't require pulling out all the acting stops, she felt as though she were merely stumbling through it. She couldn't seem to get hold of her character.

Michael was standing very close to her. Isabelle looked up at him, very aware of the shape of his mouth, the faint, thin grooves that bracketed the corners of his lips, the way his eyelashes shadowed and darkened his eyes. She forgot her next line.

She backed up slightly, and Lyle barked, "No, no, no. Don't turn away from him there, Izzy. You've got to pin him with those magnificent eyes. Like you could just suck him right in. Cassie, give her the line."

Isabelle nodded. Cassie Shumway, one of the assistant directors, prompted her, and she plunged in again. They made it through the rest of their lines. Then they moved back to their original positions to start it all over again, this time with the camera rolling.

Isabelle was miserably aware of the fact that she was not in control of the character. She did not feel as she usually did when she acted. Rather, she felt as if she were outside herself, moving somehow by remote control. She was sure that Michael must sense her nervousness. She hoped that he didn't guess why. It was absurd for a mature, experienced actress to be so nervous at the thought of an on-screen kiss. *It didn't mean anything. It wasn't real!* She was behaving like someone in junior high drama class, she told herself.

The thought served to stiffen Isabelle's spine. *She was not going to let Michael Traynor upset her so that she couldn't do her job!* She turned away, drew a deep breath and focused on the scene and her character.

When she turned back, Jessica's smolderingly sensual expression was on her face, her eyes huge and glittering, her mouth slightly pouting. When Lyle said, "Places," she took her position at the window of her apartment. The cameras began to roll. Isabelle looked around the living room, fluffing up a pillow on the couch, making sure the wine and glasses were ready, letting her face convey a subtle combination of controlled anger and determination.

The doorbell rang and she walked across the room to open it, casting a last glance of inspection down at her sexy dress and giving the neckline a little tug to make it lower. Then she wiped all the anger from her face, replacing it with a faint, almost teasing smile, and opened the door.

"Jessica." Michael stood outside, looking puzzled and impatient. "I'm here. What was so important that you couldn't discuss it on the phone?"

"Curtis... come in. Let me have your coat."

He looked for a moment as if he would refuse, then sighed and shrugged out of the overcoat, handing it to her. His eyes swept down her body, taking in the dress. "Rather... elegant for a fireside chat, aren't you?"

Heat flickered through Isabelle at the touch of Michael's gaze, and she felt a moment's panic that she was going to forget her line again. She was unaware that the inner heat showed in a softening of her lips and darkening of her mouth that was subtly seductive. When she spoke, the line coming instinctively to her mouth, her voice was slightly husky.

"Like it?" she asked, smoothing a hand over her hip and upper thigh, every curve revealed by the tight material.

"What man wouldn't?" Michael countered lightly, turning away. "But it seems a trifle formal for a chat with your future brother-in-law, that's all."

"I just got back from a party," Isabelle explained. Then she added, "Would you rather I changed into... something more comfortable?" She cocked an eyebrow and braced one hand on her hip, shooting him a challenging look.

Michael glanced at her sharply, his brows drawing together, his blue eyes hard. "No. I really haven't the time. Why don't you tell me why you asked me to come here?"

"Oh, Curtis." Isabelle pouted prettily. "You're always in such a rush. Sit down." She gave him a playful push onto the couch. "Put your feet up." She grabbed his legs and lifted them to prop his feet on the coffee table. She didn't like touching Michael, didn't like being this close. It made her feel too jumpy, too vulnerable.

He promptly put his feet back on the floor and said, irritated, "I would like to go home and get some rest. It's been a long day. Could you please get to the point?"

Ignoring his words, Isabelle walked in her signature Jessica catwalk, sleek and smooth and sexy, to a serving table where the wine and glasses stood. "Relax a little, why don't you? Have a glass of wine." She pulled the cork from the bottle and began to pour.

"I don't want any wine," he protested, but she poured it anyway and returned with the glasses.

Looking exasperated, Michael took the glass and sipped. Isabelle took a small taste of it, too, and set her glass on the coffee table, then sat down on the couch beside Michael, facing him, with her legs curled beneath her. She laid her arm along the back of the couch, her hand almost touching him. He looked at her suspiciously and shifted away from her, but was stopped by the arm of the couch.

"What is it you want?" he demanded gruffly.

"Why, Curtis, I want us to be friends."

His brows shot up. "What? That's what you called me over here for? Honestly, Jessica . . ."

He started to rise, but she planted a firm palm on his chest and pushed him back down. She did not remove her hand. Michael glanced down at her hand, then up at her, suspicion and confusion on his face.

Isabelle was very aware of the warmth of Michael's chest beneath her hand, even through his shirt. It sent strange tingles through her to touch him. Her heart was skittering, and her palms were damp. He stared at her in that long gaze so typical of soaps.

She wondered if he felt anything. It was hard to tell from the actor's mask of his face, which reflected nothing but what his character felt. But Isabelle noticed that she could feel the thud of his heart through flesh and clothes, and it was beating too hard and rapidly to be entirely normal. It gave Isabelle a curious sense of satisfaction to think that perhaps he, too, was not entirely unmoved by this enforced intimacy between them.

"Cut!" Lyle said. "Great. That was great."

Isabelle pulled back from Michael immediately and jumped up from the sofa, turning away from his bright blue gaze. Her heart was racing. She was annoyed with herself and Michael and the entire complement of writers. But, more than that, she was scared. The past scene was only the beginning of the seduction. If it had affected her this much, how was she going to make it through the rest of the day of shooting the seduction?

Numbly, she turned away.

Four

───

"Isabelle? Are you all right?" She heard Michael's voice close behind her, and then his hand was around her arm.

She stopped and looked back up at him. He was frowning down at her with concern. His fingers were warm against her bare flesh.

"What?"

"Are you feeling okay? You looked pale all of a sudden."

"Yes. I'm fine." Isabelle eased her arm out of his grasp and quickly walked away. She was glad to see that he did not try to follow her.

They had to repeat two portions of the scene so that the camera could shoot it from the other side to get the other person's reaction. Then, after a break, they blocked and rehearsed the next scene. They began to shoot.

This scene took up exactly where the other one had ended, with Isabelle's hand pressing against Michael's chest to keep him from rising. She scooted closer to him on the couch.

"Don't go," she said huskily. Remembering what Lyle had instructed her, she turned the full force of her eyes upon Michael. "I mean, since we're both so close to Mark, it doesn't make sense that we should argue. We ought to be together, to... unite to help him however we can."

"If you're trying to convince me to persuade him not to go on the medical mission," Michael said, his voice a trifle uneven, "you can forget it. It's what he wants, and it's a wonderful project. I'm not going to use my influence with Mark to keep him from doing something that means so much to him."

Isabelle's hand moved slowly up Michael's chest to the hollow of his throat. "I'm not asking you to do that," she assured him softly, her eyes never leaving his. "I just want us to be friends."

Now her fingers trailed down the middle of his shirt, lingering over each button. Michael gazed into her eyes, seemingly unable to tear his gaze away. His breath came harder and faster.

"There's no reason for us to be enemies," Isabelle went on in a low, sexy voice, and as she talked, she moved her face closer and closer to his. "Come on. Can't we kiss and make up?"

She leaned forward to kiss him. For an instant, his face moved toward hers, too, but then he stopped and grasped her shoulders with his hands, thrusting her away from him. He jumped up and walked away to the window, then whirled around.

"What in the hell do you think you're pulling, Jessica?"

"I don't know what you mean," Isabelle replied, visibly smoothing the irritation from her face. She left the sofa and slinked across the set toward Michael. "Why are you so jumpy?"

"I'm not jumpy. But you were..." He gestured toward the couch.

"I was what?" she asked, rounding her eyes innocently.

He glared at her. "You know exactly what you were doing, but I'll feel like a fool if I say it." He released a long breath. "I'd better go."

"No. Please. We haven't finished talking."

Michael grimaced. "I think we've more than finished. I don't know what you're trying to do, but it won't work. This is one man who doesn't fall for your wiles."

"Oh, really? And why is that?" Isabelle smiled, and she ran her eyes slowly down his body. "Funny, you look like you'd be fully...functional." She cocked an eyebrow teasingly.

He stiffened, and his eyes sparked, but then he raised his hands as if holding something back and said, "No. You're not going to get to me that way, either."

"Why, whatever do you mean?" Isabelle moved closer, and Michael did not step back. She was only inches away from him, and she gazed deeply into his eyes. "I think that you must have misunderstood what I said." She began to play idly with one of the middle buttons of his shirt.

"I don't think so." His voice came out a little choked, and he moved back.

"What's the matter, Curtis? Scared of me?" Isabelle's expression was mocking and filled with sexual challenge. Holding his eyes with hers, she laid her palms flat against his chest and slid her hands slowly upward.

Michael swallowed hard, and his jaw clenched, but he did not step away.

"No, not scared." His voice was husky. "Just curious."

"Curious?" She repeated without much interest. All her attention was now focused on his mouth. She moved across the inches that separated them so that their bodies were now lightly touching. The heat of Michael's body blazed through Isabelle's body like an electric shock, and she knew that her face was now soft with sensuality, her eyes dark and beckoning, without the least bit of effort on her part.

"Curious about what?" she murmured, linking her hands behind his neck. She turned up her face, offering up her succulent mouth to be kissed. "What it would feel like to kiss me?" Her lips were only a breath away from his now. Her heart was racing, and heat was pooling in her abdomen. "To take me to bed?"

Michael drew in his breath sharply, and his arms wrapped up around her. His mouth sank into hers. He kissed her hungrily, and whatever heat Isabelle had felt before was like nothing compared to the explosion that tore through her body now. His lips were hot and firm, pressing into her, moving her own lips apart. His arms molded her against him. She could feel every solid, muscular inch of his body against hers, and her loins blossomed with heat.

It had been so many years since she had kissed him that she had forgotten how it felt—how hot and fierce his mouth was, how sweet and yet demanding. She had forgotten the hungry, yearning way he wrapped himself around her, as if he would pull her into him and consume her. A shudder ran through her, and she tightened her arms convulsively around his neck.

Finally he raised his head, and for a long moment they stared into each other's eyes. Then, in a flash of embarrassment, awareness of where they were came back to Isabelle, and she could see from the look in his eyes that Michael, too, had joltingly returned to reality. He drew in a breath, and then he released her, putting his hands on her shoulders and setting her away from him.

"No," he said in a rough voice. "I wasn't curious about that. I just wanted to see how far you would be willing to go to get what you want." He quirked an eyebrow coldly. "I guess I found out."

Isabelle's eyes flashed, and her hand lashed out to slap him. They had rehearsed it, but earlier she had not moved with such quickness and venom. Still, he caught her wrist, just as planned, and held her arm motionless.

"Don't try to take me on, Jessica," he warned her. "I promise you, that's one fight you'll lose."

He stepped back, dropping her arm, and turned and walked away from her. Isabelle stared after him in outrage and shock. As he reached the door, she broke out of her paralysis and, letting out a shriek, grabbed up a vase from a nearby table. She hurled it toward him, and it hit the wall with a satisfying crash. He was gone by then, but she picked up a book from the table and sent it flying after him. It hit the door with a thud. She sent all the loose pillows of the couch after the book and then flung herself down on the sofa in a paroxysm of rage.

"Damn you, Curtis Townsend!" she hissed fiercely. "I'll get you for this! Whatever it takes, I'll get you!"

Isabelle curled up in the chair in her dressing room, her knees pulled up to her chest and her arms wrapped around them. She laid her cheek against one knee and closed her eyes. She wished she could close her mind, as well, but that kept playing over the earlier scene with Michael. Her cheeks flushed again, just thinking of it. He had known—he had to have known—how quickly and deeply she had responded to his kiss. She had had no perspective, no distance, at all. She had reacted as if Michael were kissing her, not Curtis kissing Jessica. He could not have mistaken the rush of heat throughout her body or the eager way her mouth had pressed back against his. He knew that she had wanted him, as she had years before. No doubt he thought that she would be just as easy pickings for him as she had been then—provided he wanted to take her.

She wondered if the director and crew had recognized the reality of the desire, too. She prayed they weren't all snickering behind her back at the way she had practically melted when Michael kissed her. She could only hope that they would simply assume that it was one of Jessica's typical overheated scenes. The character had, after all, been married three times—twice to the same man—and had several affairs. Sex was Jessica's usual weapon. If she was lucky, they wouldn't notice the difference between the fake kisses, choreographed by her and the other actor, that were normal for Jessica's love scenes, and the spontaneous combustion that had ignited today. She hated to think of the jokes that she would be subjected to if they had picked up on the difference.

There was a knock on the door, and Isabelle called listlessly, "Come in."

The door opened, and Isabelle, her head down on her knees and her face turned from the door, gestured vaguely toward the opposite wall. "It's hanging up over there."

"I'm not Wardrobe," a man's voice answered.

Isabelle's head snapped up and she stared in horror. "Michael!" She glanced down instinctively at herself. She was wearing only an old front-closing robe she often wore between changes or in Makeup. Three of the buttons were missing, and it was short enough that much of her legs were exposed—especially sitting as she was. Quickly she put her legs down and tugged the robe into place around them.

"What are you doing here?" she asked exasperatedly.

"Thank you. Nice to see you, too," he replied sarcastically.

"Well? It isn't exactly as if we're friends."

"What are we, then, exactly? I have to tell you, I got a little confused today on the set."

Isabelle's cheeks flooded with red and she looked away.

"The day I first came to the show, and I tried to talk to you, you acted like I had crawled out from under a rock," he went on. "I figured, okay, if that's the way you wanted it, that's the way I'd play it. I mean, I know you have a right to resent me...."

"Resent you!" Isabelle cast him a scornful glance. "Despise is more like it."

He looked at her evenly for a moment, then said, "All right. Despise me, then. No doubt I deserve that. Anyway, I stayed away from you, didn't even talk to you off the set because I thought it was what you wanted. Then, today..."

"Today what?" Isabelle faced him, brazening it out.

"You know what. When I kissed you, it was like it was before with us. It was all I could do to stop and say my lines. All I wanted to do was keep kissing you."

Isabelle turned away, and Michael reached out and grasped her shoulder, turning her back. He loomed above her, his eyes boring into hers.

"Don't tell me you didn't feel it, too," he went on in a low voice.

"Don't be absurd," Isabelle replied breathlessly. "I was acting! We were supposed to kiss, so I kissed you the way my character would. That's all."

"You expect me to believe that? You mean to tell me you kiss every man you play a scene with like you're going to melt and flow all over his skin?"

"Stop it! Don't say that!"

"Why? Because it's the truth? Damn it, Isabelle, why are you pretending?"

"I'm not pretending!" Isabelle blazed back, frightened by the weakness she felt at his touch. In another moment, he would be kissing her again to prove his point, and she didn't think that she could stand that. "It was a scene, nothing more. I was acting. Anything I felt was only what my character would have felt."

Michael released her shoulder, but he remained where he was, watching her. Isabelle kept her eyes turned away from him, unable to meet his gaze.

Finally he said, "You're lying. I just don't know whether you're lying to me . . . or to yourself."

"Please. Go away and leave me alone."

Michael let out a sigh, then turned and left the dressing room. Isabelle collapsed into her chair and buried her face in her hands.

"I don't know if I can continue to do it," Isabelle said, picking up the glass carafe of coffee and carrying it into the small breakfast room where her friend sat. "I mean, it's so hard to face him day after day."

"You haven't had to kiss him again, have you?" Nancy asked, raising her cup to her lips.

Nancy was sitting in her customary loose, casual fashion, her long legs draped over one arm of the chair and her thin torso sideways in the seat. Her long mop of thick golden-red curls tumbled haphazardly around her face, the result of her having just run her hands through her hair. Nancy Baker had been Isabelle's best friend for years. They had met when Isabelle had first come to Hollywood, and Nancy had been the fledgling photographer who had taken Isabelle's photographs for her portfolio. They had shared both a professional relationship and a close friendship ever since.

Nancy was the one person to whom Isabelle felt she could tell anything without fear of it ever being repeated or judged. Nor was Nancy intimidated by or jealous of Isabelle's good looks. She had been a successful model before she became a photographer, and she understood the problems of being known to the world as a beautiful face. But perhaps the thing that had most cemented their friendship was the fact that Nancy accepted Jenny with complete equanimity; her younger brother had been born with Down's syndrome and had always been a beloved part of their family.

Nancy and Isabelle had gone shopping together this morning while Irma stayed with Jenny. Now they were enjoying a friendly cup of coffee and a long talk while they kept an eye on Jenny and the dog wheeling around in the concrete driveway and parking area.

"No," Isabelle admitted, adding, "thank heavens. But every week I've had more scenes with him. It's been three weeks since that seduction scene, and next week I have at least one scene with him every day."

Nancy shrugged. "You knew you would have to work with the guy."

"You don't understand. When he came to the show, Curtis and Jessica had virtually no relationship. But the writers keep building it up."

"Why?"

Isabelle shrugged. "The other day Judy Weinburg told me that she loved getting to write a scene for Jessica with a man who wasn't one of her former husbands or a past or present lover or someone who was trying to get into bed with her."

Nancy hooted. "That makes sense. Jessica is the Slut of the World."

Isabelle made a face. "Anyway, I don't think that's it, or at least, not all of it. It's worse. I have the awful feeling they're going to try to cook something up between Curtis and Jessica."

Nancy raised her eyebrows. "Aha. The plot thickens. Why do you think that?"

"Because Danny Archer absolutely loved the seduction scene. He says it's one everyone will be wishing they'd videotaped. Secondly, the actor that played Mark took a month's leave of absence. He left a week ago. So, for the next three weeks, they have nothing much to do with Jessica. Thirdly, Lena, whom they had pegged to be Curtis's love interest, isn't creating much of a spark with him. Fan mail, so I hear, has been very tepid."

"Well, if the fans don't love him, then maybe they'll get rid of him altogether."

"Fat chance. *He* gets lots of fan mail. Everyone from grandmothers down to giggly adolescent girls thinks he's a major hunk. They keep writing in to say don't pair him with that drip Celeste. That's Lena's character."

"So they're going to try to pair him with you?"

"I don't know. I haven't asked. Half the women on the show would love to be a couple with him, but most of them are either the wrong age or they're already hooked up with someone."

"So is Jessica."

Isabelle rolled her eyes. "It doesn't matter if Jessica is hooked up with someone. Anyway, the seduction scene aired last Monday. There's a three-week lag between shooting and showing it. Friday, Marie showed me the pile of mail they've already gotten about it."

"Did they like it or hate it?"

"Both. Some of them were incensed, and others thought it was great. And I quote, 'It showed the wild, sexy side of that gorgeous Dr. Townsend.' Either way, it's viewer response, and that's what the producers care about. That's what brings in ad money. Whether they loved it or hated it, the viewers will be watching to see what happens."

"Oh."

"Yeah, 'oh.' Tuesday, Karen—the head writer—was closeted with Danny and Carol half the day. Wednesday and Thursday, she and two or three of the writers were in her office all day. Something is obviously up. The rumor is that they're changing one of the story lines. I mean, majorly changing. And Carol's secretary says she canceled all the reservations for the location shooting in New Orleans in two weeks."

"Really? What are they going to do, then?"

Isabelle shrugged. "At the moment, no one knows. Maybe they've called it off altogether. Maybe they're doing it somewhere else. Maybe they just decided it was going to rain too much in New Orleans—or maybe they've scrapped the story and are going to do something entirely different."

"I bet everybody's buzzing about that."

"Oh!" Isabelle rolled her eyes. "Sets are always such rumor mills, anyway. Now stories are circulating all over the place. Who knows what's true and what's just speculation."

Nancy studied her coffee for a moment. "What will you do if it is true? If they're going to link you and him in a long story line?"

"I don't know! I don't think I can stand it! But how can I leave, either? Just drop a steady job and endanger Jenny's security, not to mention my career? It isn't even as if I could do it easily. They could sue me for not finishing my contract."

"Well, it sounded as if Traynor gave in quickly enough when you made it plain you didn't want anything happening between you. Maybe he won't push it, even if you are doing steamy scenes on stage."

"Maybe...." Isabelle got up and walked restlessly to the window. She stood for a moment, looking out at her daughter. The problem, Isabelle knew, wasn't so much that she was afraid that Michael would bother her because of their steamy scenes. The problem was that she wasn't sure whether she could hold out against her own desires. She was afraid that if they kissed again on-screen, she wouldn't be able to stop.

But that was something she could not admit to anyone, even her best friend. She turned back to Nancy, forcing a smile. "You're probably right. I'm worrying for nothing. Who knows—they may not even decide to throw Curtis and Jessica together. It's all rumors and speculations, anyway. Let's talk about something else."

"Sure." Nancy readily complied, moving on to the subject of her next showing at a gallery.

* * *

However, the next week, Isabelle's fears were confirmed. Carol Nieman sent for her. Carol was the assistant producer for "Tomorrows," and she did most of the actual management of the show. Danny Archer, the producer, also produced another soap, and he oversaw both operations. The way it usually worked out was that Danny took the credit when something went very well and dumped the blame on Carol whenever anything went wrong.

When Isabelle stepped into her office, Carol looked up at her, smiling, and said, "How does a trip to Cancún sound to you?"

Isabelle gazed back, uncomprehending. "What? A trip to Cancún? I don't understand."

"We've decided to scrap the location shoot in New Orleans. I guess you've heard about that."

Isabelle nodded, and Carol shook her head and sighed. "It's almost impossible to keep anything secret on this set."

Isabelle refrained from pointing out that a change in secretaries might help stop the flow of rumors. After all, she had no desire to end the actors' pipeline. She merely tried to look agreeably sympathetic.

"Sit down. Sit down," Carol said, waving toward one of the chairs in front of her desk. "Well, at least you haven't heard it all, obviously. We've decided instead of New Orleans, to go on location to Cancún for a week. Different story line. And you're going to be one of the actors going on location." She smiled beneficently, as one bestowing a great favor.

"Really?" Isabelle tried to look appropriately appreciative, but her heart sank. "Who else?"

"Not many people. Just a couple of day players and you and Michael Traynor."

"Oh." Isabelle's voice came out hoarse. She cleared her throat and forced a creaky smile onto her face. It was even worse than she had feared. Obviously they were linking her story line with Michael's. But worse than that, she was going to have to spend a week in Cancún with Michael!

Five

———

Isabelle glanced over at Lyle, who was busily flipping back and forth between his copy of the script and the shooting schedule, making notes. She then turned her head back to the window, gazing at the blue sea beneath them. The plane was obviously dropping lower and lower. It wouldn't be long before they'd set down in Cancún.

She sighed and turned back to the seat in front of her. Everyone except herself, of course, was delighted with the new story line. Even Lyle, normally the gloomiest of men, was patently enthused. He had spent almost the entire flight working on the various scenes they were to film, as engrossed as if they were his first scenes as a director. What time he hadn't been working, he had been talking to Isabelle about the new story line.

Isabelle could understand everyone's enthusiasm. If it hadn't been Michael Traynor involved, she would have been interested, too. They were taking a new direction from the one that both Isabelle's character and the show had been following the past two or three years. "Tomorrows" had always been primarily a character show, its story lines built slowly on the complications of the characters' entanglements with each other. Most of the villainy done had been either financial finaglings or romantic schemes. Jessica, naturally, had been involved in both. The new story line infused new blood in the form of physical action and a nastier, more personal villainy, as well as a different sort of story for Jessica.

The past two weeks of scripts had had Jessica and Curtis becoming more and more worried about Mark Townsend, from whom they had heard no word. Finally they had learned that his medical mission in Central America had been attacked by guerrillas. No one knew anything about the survivors, and Curtis had decided to fly down to the fictitious country of San Pedro to investigate Mark's disappearance for himself. Jessica had insisted on coming, too, despite Curtis's objections.

The location shooting would be of the two of them traveling to the mission and searching for Mark. Cancún and its environs would substitute for San Pedro. When they returned to L.A., they would do the interior shots and add them for the month-long story that would dominate the May sweeps. By that time, Jim Ehrlich, the actor who played Mark, would have returned, and they would add scenes of his captivity by, and ultimate escape from, the new villain whom they were bringing onto the show.

There would be a great deal more action scenes, not only with Mark fighting off his captors and escaping—though pursued back to the U.S. by the villain—but also of Curtis and Jessica eluding guerrilla fighters and the army, as well as henchmen of the new, as yet only hinted-at, villain. At first, Curtis and Jessica would engage in their customary bickering, and there would be some funny scenes about Jessica's exasperating concern with her luggage and her attire. Then, during a harrowing ride in a Jeep, they were to have a wreck and Curtis would strike his head hard on the windshield.

Jessica would then have to take charge of their escape from their pursuers. Normally, Isabelle, too, would have been excited about this story, which presented new challenges for her. For one thing, Jessica would have an opportunity to use her considerable skills for a good purpose. It would also lift her out of her usual shallow concerns over her looks, dress and money. That would give Isabelle an opportunity to explore new facets of her character.

But Isabelle could not enjoy the creative opportunities the story offered because of the romantic relationship that it created between Jessica and Curtis Townsend. When Curtis would come to from his injury, not only would he be in pain, he would also be suffering from amnesia. He would not know who he was, who Jessica was, where they were or what they were doing there. Jessica, of course, would have a dazzling opportunity to take advantage of his lack of memory. Curtis would assume, since they were together, that they are friends, perhaps even lovers, and Jessica wickedly would go along with this assumption. One of the location shots would be a love scene by a lagoon in the jungle. It was a titillating scene, much longer than Jessica's previous attempt at seduction, and involving a good deal of simulated kissing and caressing.

The problem for Isabelle, of course, was how little of the scene would need to be simulated. Thinking about it now, she gritted her teeth. She could not afford to let herself get carried away this time. She had to remain cool, calm and professional, unaffected by any base desires.

Now below her she could see land, the dense growth of the Yucatán Peninsula. The plane was dropping ever lower, obviously coming in for a landing. Isabelle's ears popped, and she thought about Jenny, as she usually did when she was taking off or landing in an airplane. In general, she was not afraid of flying, but she had read somewhere that the majority of airplane accidents happened right after takeoff or right before landing, and over the years she had come to dread those moments a little and to think of her daughter.

She thought of Jenny's little face, the dark slash of eyebrows and the vivid blue color of her eyes, so similar to her father's. She remembered Jenny's grave expression and the way she had hugged her when Isabelle left for the airport this morning. Irma Pena would take good care of her for a week and be very patient with Jenny's repeated questions of where her mother was and what she was doing and when she would be back. And, of course, Isabelle would phone her every night.

Isabelle closed her eyes. There was the bump that signified that they were on the ground, and she was able to relax. She glanced over at Lyle, a trifle embarrassed that he might have seen her moment of apprehension. To her relief, Lyle was busily packing up his things in his briefcase. Her eyes slid across the aisle, and she found herself gazing into Michael's face. He was watching her, and she realized with annoyance that *he* had probably witnessed her nervous reaction.

Michael smiled, but there was no mockery in his face, only a faint warmth, even sympathy. He winked, and Isabelle's heart gave a lurch. Though long-forgotten, that wink was instantly familiar, and the warmth it spread through her body was only partly a reaction to unexpected kindness. Isabelle looked away quickly.

When the plane taxied up to the terminal and stopped, Isabelle waited for Lyle to get his briefcase and bag together, then exited behind him. Michael stood waiting politely for them to pass in front of him before he stepped out into the aisle, so that Isabelle wound up sandwiched between him and Lyle. She was very conscious of Michael's long, lean body behind her, especially when the crowd of disembarking passengers swelled frontward, pushing him intimately close to her back. She was relieved when the door opened and the people in front of her started off the plane, so that she could move away from the warm pressure of Michael's body.

They moved into the small, modern airport and waited through a short line for Customs, then walked out into the bright Mexican sunshine. A limousine waited to take Isabelle, Lyle and Michael to their hotel. The crew, with their expensive cameras, film and other gear, would take a longer time to get through Customs and would be following later, along with the day players, in two vans.

The heat was immediate and pervasive, the sunlight dazzling. Isabelle slid into the dark, air-conditioned limousine gratefully. Michael and Lyle came in after her, Lyle sitting on the far end of the wide, plush seat where Isabelle was. Michael, after a quick glance at the empty expanse of seat between Isabelle and Lyle, took one of the fold-down side seats. Isabelle noticed he had more or less done the same thing on the airplane this morning, insisting that Lyle take the seat beside Isabelle while he took the seat across the aisle by himself. She wondered if he was being sensitive to her feelings or if he wanted to be close to her as little as she wanted to be close to him. She suspected that it was the former, and she was grateful to him for his gesture. But at the same time, it left an odd, empty feeling in her.

Impatiently, she thrust the thought away from her. She was only feeling the sense of loss she experienced anytime she was away from her daughter for more than a day. It had nothing to do with Michael Traynor. Isabelle turned and gazed out the window at the landscape, thickly grown with scrubby brush and trees. There were no people or buildings in sight, only a road sign or a billboard now and then. Lyle was talking about the schedule tomorrow, but she paid little attention to him. Cassie, his assistant, would bring a photocopy of the schedule tonight, and until then Lyle might change it, so there was little point in learning it yet.

They drove across a bridge, and a few moments later they were suddenly back in civilization. Hotels, sprawling or tall and narrow, were clustered along the right side of the road, and every once in a while, Isabelle caught a glimpse of the ocean surf pounding upon the shore. She decided she'd take a walk along the beach this evening. Perhaps here she would not be recognized, especially if she wore a beach hat and sunglasses.

Their hotel was a typical resort hotel, with cool tiled-and-marbled floors and, between the building and the beach, a meandering pool built to look like a tropical stream, except for the swim-up bar thrusting out into the middle of it. Her room, also tiled, was pleasant, colorfully decorated and there was a long balcony off it that looked out over the ocean. Two chairs and a small table sat on the balcony, and potted plants had been set in the two front corners. A large pottery vase decorated one of the inside corners.

Isabelle went out onto the balcony and stood at the railing, drawing in a long breath of satisfaction. She loved the smell and sight of the ocean. In the past, she had considered moving to a house on the beach, but she had worried about Jenny wandering away from the house and into the ocean. Jenny could swim in a pool and enjoyed theirs very much, but the ocean was something else again. When they went to the beach, Isabelle was careful to be with her the whole time. It would be too easy for Jenny to get caught in an undertow and panic.

Isabelle leaned against the railing, watching a boat towing a parasail. The sail was hot pink, a bright splash of color against the clear blue sky, and the rider dangled beneath it, looking much too small and vulnerable.

There was the sound of a patio door sliding open, and Isabelle turned her head toward the neighboring balcony. A waist-high metal railing separated the two balconies, and Isabelle could see the occupant of the other room clearly as he stepped out onto his balcony. It was Michael. Isabelle's mouth tightened in irritation.

Michael glanced over at her. "Oh, hello. I didn't realize anyone was out here."

"Hello." Isabelle's enjoyment of the view was spoiled now. However, it seemed too rude and too childish to duck back into her room just because Michael had come onto his balcony. *Why did they have to be next door to each other?*

As if sensing her thought, Michael smiled slightly and said, "They've put us all together. Lyle's on the other side of you. And they put Jackson over there." He named the cameraman, nodding toward the balcony that lay on the other side of his. "Makeup, Wardrobe, everything... we're all up and down this hall."

"I see." She shrugged, indicating her indifference. "I guess it doesn't matter."

"I suppose not."

Isabelle turned back toward her door. "Well, I think I'll go take a nap now."

She went quickly back inside, closing the heavy drapes against the sunlight and the sight of Michael, arms braced on the railing of his balcony, looking out over the ocean. She felt trapped. It seemed as if everything and everyone was conspiring to throw her together with Michael. With a groan of disgust, she threw herself on her bed and closed her eyes. *How in the world was she going to make it through the next week?*

It was hot, and Isabelle was damp with perspiration. She was lying on a lounge chair on the beach; she could hear the ocean rolling in to shore near her, a muted, constant background. She was utterly alone; the beach was deserted.

She opened her eyes, and she saw Michael standing there, looking down at her. He wore only a towel around his waist, and his flesh was bronzed and gleaming. Heat flared in her abdomen as she looked up at him. He knelt beside her chair and, without saying a word, he slid his hand down her body, silently, almost lazily, exploring every curve and crevice. Isabelle's breasts swelled and ached in response, and her nipples tightened, pointing against the material of her bikini top. He caressed her stomach and abdomen, and his fingers slipped between her legs to rub softly up and down, touching her through the material of her swimsuit. She was flooded with moisture at his touch. She stretched sensuously and opened her legs wider, reveling in the pleasure.

*Then, somehow, her swimsuit was gone, and she was
completely naked. The sun was hot upon her skin, but
not as hot as Michael's eyes and hands. He caressed her
everywhere, never saying a word as his fingers searched
her most intimate spots. Isabelle wanted to touch him,
too, but somehow she could not. It was frustrating, but
the intense pleasure overrode that. His finger slipped inside her, stroking in and out, and she moved with him,
raising her pelvis from the bed. He took her nipple in his
mouth as his fingers found the fleshy little nub between
her legs and began to stroke it. Isabelle gasped as his
mouth and finger worked in unison, arousing her. Her
hips moved frantically, seeking release. Then the explosion came, so hard it woke her up.*

Isabelle opened her eyes, staring blankly up at the
ceiling. Her loins were like melted wax, and there was a
sweet pulsation between her legs. She squeezed her legs
together reflexively, but it didn't satisfy her. She wanted
to feel his fullness inside her.

She groaned and rolled over, burying her face in her
pillow. She was flushed with pleasure, yet at the same
time strangely dissatisfied. *It wasn't enough.* The dream
had left her hot and tingling, aching for the reality of
Michael's touch. She wanted to feel his kiss, his touch,
the weight of his body on hers.

With a low curse, Isabelle stood up and went into the
bathroom to splash cool water on her face. She didn't
know how she would be able to face Michael again after
that dream. She was afraid that every time she'd look at
him, she would remember the wanton way she had responded to him in the dream. He would know nothing of
it, but she knew it would embarrass her. Worse than that,
she was afraid she could not look at him without wanting to feel all the glorious sensations she had experi-

enced in the dream. Now, more than ever, she wondered how she was going to last through this filming. The week ahead seemed unbearable—especially the love scene they would be filming in a day or two!

Isabelle changed her clothes and went for a brisk walk on the beach, hoping that would clear the sensual thoughts from her head. It was only partially successful. She ate supper alone on the terrace overlooking the ocean and went to bed early. But as soon as her head touched the pillow, the memory of her dream came flooding back, filling her mind, and it was a long time before she finally fell asleep.

The next morning she arose early, as they all had to, and ate breakfast in the hotel café with Debbie and Callie, the hairstylist and makeup artist. They were the only other women from the show on the location shoot. Both the women were nice, and generally Isabelle found their conversation interesting enough, but this morning their chatter merely irritated her. Their main topic of conversation was Michael Traynor, who walked into the restaurant while they were eating. He smiled and stopped by the table to say hello, then made his way to his table, stopping with a gracious smile to sign an autograph for an adoring fan.

Callie sighed and said, "He is *so* yummy."

"Why is everyone so gaga over him?" Isabelle asked sourly.

Debbie gaped at her. "You mean you don't like him?"

"Not much." Isabelle shrugged. "He's handsome, but..."

"Oh, he's a lot more than that. He's nice, too," Debbie assured her. "I mean, he's not a stuck-up mannequin, like Brooks Fitzgerald was."

Isabelle groaned. Brooks had played her first husband on the show and had been immensely popular with the viewers, but he had been a constant source of irritation to everyone who had to work with him. Almost the whole cast and crew, not to mention the writers, had heaved a collective sigh of relief when he had left the show.

"No one's like Brooks."

"Yeah, but Michael's different from lots of them. He doesn't just turn your knees to water. He's friendly and polite and...well, treats you like a regular person. Whenever I'm doing his makeup, he asks me about my little boy."

"Don't you like him, Isabelle?" Callie asked, her expression almost worried. "In that seduction scene, you two looked like you got along pretty well."

"That was acting," Isabelle replied promptly.

"Well, it was *some* acting, then."

"You aren't at all interested in him?" Debbie added. "I mean, both of you being single and all. And if you set off sparks like that just acting..."

"No," Isabelle replied firmly, standing up and laying her napkin down on the table. "I am not at all interested in him. Sorry, I have to run now. I've got to go over the script again."

She started away, but as she did so, she overheard Debbie whisper to Callie, "Well, I'm still betting on them getting together."

She came to a dead stop and listened as Callie agreed, "Yeah, me, too. I think she's protesting too much."

Isabelle turned back around. The two women glanced up and saw her, and their faces flooded with guilt. Isabelle took the two steps back to the table.

"What are you talking about? Is there a bet on the show about us?" There was a great deal of tedium involved in producing a television show, and it was often relieved on "Tomorrows" by practical jokes and bets on all sorts of events.

"Well...yes," Debbie replied reluctantly.

"How could you!" Isabelle's face flushed with anger. "That's an invasion of privacy. What gives you all the right to bet on my love life?"

Callie defended herself. "Everyone does it. You bet on Phil's baby last year."

"There's a good deal of difference between betting on whether a baby will be a boy or a girl and betting on whether someone goes to bed with someone else!"

"Only in degree," Debbie affirmed. "You can't keep people from being curious about it after that scene between the two of you."

"It was just a scene!" Isabelle snapped. "Why can't anybody realize that?"

"Because your love scenes with Jim never steam up the cameras," Callie replied bluntly.

"It didn't mean anything. I am *not* interested in Michael Traynor! And you can tell all your buddies that they're wasting their money if they're betting on us going to bed with each other."

She turned on her heel and stalked off, leaving the two women gazing after her thoughtfully. They looked back at each other.

"Who said anything about going to bed with each other?" Callie asked. "The bet's just for a date, isn't it?"

"Yes." Debbie grinned suddenly. "I think that's what's called a Freudian slip. I believe I'll double my bet."

They spent the morning shooting a beach scene in which Jessica and Curtis argued in their usual biting way and which ended with Jessica pouring a tall glass of a tropical drink into Curtis's lap. Isabelle derived a great deal of satisfaction from doing it; it banished the nasty mood she'd been in all morning.

The AD gushed about how wonderful Isabelle's wickedly gloating expression was. Isabelle wondered if the girl had money down on the opposite side—that she and Michael wouldn't get together. The thought struck her as amusing, and after that she could not recapture the indignation she had felt earlier. When Callie pleaded for her not to be mad during the afternoon makeup session, Isabelle had to smile and shrug the whole thing off.

In the afternoon, they shot an exterior scene in town where she and Michael came running out of the front of a shop and down the street after a man who had offered them information about Mark's whereabouts. After that, they shot two more scenes of them chasing the man through the maze of stalls that made up the open-air market. They finished the day with sunset shots of Michael walking along the beach, looking troubledly out at the ocean and of Isabelle standing on the terrace of the hotel, watching Michael.

The next morning they were up at dawn to ride out in the vans to shoot the car chase scenes. They were to be shot on a side road that led to a small beach from the main highway. The road had been blocked off at the highway. While the crew set up to shoot, Michael strolled over to the nearby beach, and Isabelle went into the deserted tropical juice bar. She sat down at one of the empty tables to wait. As she sat, idly watching the crew work, dark clouds massed on the horizon and moved toward them. Suddenly, wind was whipping through the open-air building in which Isabelle sat, and the skies opened up, sending down a torrential tropical rain.

The crew and director jumped into the vans down beside the shoot. Isabelle settled back in her chair to wait out the storm alone. Then Michael came running up from the beach and into the bar. He was already drenched, his thick hair dripping water and his shirt plastered to his muscular body. He swept his hands back through his hair, squeezing out the water, and glanced around.

"Well," he said, taking note of the empty building, "looks like we're stranded here together."

Six

_____

Isabelle was reminded forcibly of her dream from two days before, and she flushed, her mind suddenly flooded with images from the dream. Her mouth was dry, and she was incapable of saying anything.

Michael walked over to Isabelle's table and grasped the back of one of the cane chairs. Grinning down at her, he asked, "Do you think you can stand being alone with me? Or shall I sit across the room?"

His joking words made Isabelle feel foolish, bringing her joltingly back to reality, and she said ungraciously, "No. Sit down."

"Why, thank you." He ran his hand down his face and over his hair again, sluicing the water from himself, then sat down in the chair. He pulled the wet shirt away from his body, looking down at it ruefully. "Callie'll be on my case about soaking this shirt. I'm supposed to be crisp and pressed when we start out." His wry smile invited her to join in his amusement at his own sorry state. "A Townsend would never look like a drowned rat, after all."

"It'll dry soon enough when the sun comes out," Isabelle replied unsympathetically. "Besides, I don't imagine Callie would scold you even if you'd dragged your shirt through the mud."

He raised an eyebrow at her remark. "What's that supposed to mean?"

"That every female member of the office staff and crew and cast practically swoon over you."

"Not *every* one," he replied, looking pointedly at Isabelle.

She shrugged and turned her head to gaze out at the rain. Michael, shivering a little as the wind swept over his wet body, stared stonily in the same direction for a few minutes.

Finally Isabelle broke the silence. Still staring straight ahead of her, she asked in a determinedly casual voice, "Did you know that they're making bets on us?"

Michael glanced at her, puzzled. "Bets? On us? What do you mean?"

"You know. Surely you've made them. A few years ago, everyone was betting on whether Sandra Fein would go through with her wedding. She'd been engaged three times, and the others all fell through."

"I see." He looked at her profile for a moment, then said quietly, "And what are they betting about us?"

"Whether we'll get together." She looked at him. "You didn't know anything about it?"

"First I'd heard of it. But, then, I suppose you and I would be the last to know."

"Obviously it doesn't bother you."

Michael shrugged. "What's to bother me? They're just amusing themselves, and it doesn't hurt me any." He studied her. "Why does it bother you?"

"I don't like people poking their noses in my private life."

"I presume they aren't spying on us all the time to find out."

"I don't know. I wouldn't put it past them," Isabelle said darkly.

He chuckled. "Come on, I think you're reaching for that." He paused, then went on, "It's because they're linking us together, isn't it? You don't like that even in jest."

There was another long silence. Isabelle refused to let herself turn and look at Michael. Finally he said, his voice low and husky with emotion, "You know, Isabelle, I never wanted to hurt you. I'm sorry. I wish I could take back what I did to you then."

Isabelle crossed her arms over her body. "You don't need to apologize. I was young and stupid. I should never have gotten involved with you."

"I know. I knew it then. You were too young. Hell, I was too young. I tried not to fall for you. You probably don't believe that, but I did. I knew you were too innocent for me. But I—whenever I was around you, I didn't have much luck keeping my head. I told myself it wouldn't hurt to be around you, to talk to you. Then that wasn't enough. I had to be alone with you. Of course, that wasn't enough, either. Nothing was enough until you were in my bed "

Isabelle's body contracted involuntarily at the sensual picture his words conjured up, and heat stole through her as she remembered that first night . . . the two of them lying close together in Michael's narrow bed, his heat enveloping her, his hands drifting over her body.

"Then I couldn't stop," Michael went on baldly. "Once I'd known that pleasure, been so close to you, a part of you, I couldn't give it up."

Isabelle hated the warmth flooding through her, hated the fact that he could stir her with nothing more than his voice. She stiffened against the treacherous feeling, tightening her mouth into a thin line.

"Stop it!" Isabelle snapped, whirling to face him. She intended to say more, to cut him with her words until he withdrew from her table. But the sight of his face, warm and soft with sensuality, stopped her. For an instant, she could not breathe.

This time, it was he who looked away. "God! When you look at me, I want to..." Michael drew a long, shuddering breath. "I never dreamed that you could still do the same thing to me. I thought when I took this job that we could put the past behind us, that maybe somehow we could even be friends."

"I think that's impossible," Isabelle said in a choked voice.

"You're right about that." Michael ran his hands over his face. "Oh, hell." He rose to his feet, shoving his chair back abruptly. He started to walk away, but then he turned and leaned down, bracing his hands on the table and staring directly into her face. "I want you to know one thing. You seem to think that I just tossed you aside like an old shirt or something, that I walked away without a backward glance or the slightest twinge of pain. But let me tell you, I lay awake at night, thinking about you and sweating, wanting you so bad, I thought I'd do almost anything to make it stop. I hated myself for leaving you, for making you suffer, for making me suffer. I picked up the phone so many times and called you, but then I'd hang up. Once I even got on a train and rode halfway to Virginia before I came to my senses and got off and went back. You were not a few casual nights in the sack for me. I loved you. And when I left, it hurt like hell."

Isabelle gazed at him, bereft of speech. Michael pushed himself away from the table and walked to the other side of the bar, where he stood, arms crossed, leaning against one of the supporting posts, staring out at the rain.

Isabelle stared at his back, struggling to pull her scattered thoughts together. Michael's words had hit her like stones, painful in their intensity. For a moment she was stunned. Then a variety of emotions began to well up in her—sympathy, bewilderment, even guilt and a strange longing to comfort him. A saving anger swelled up in her, sweeping away the other emotions. *The nerve of him, to try to make her feel sorry for him, when he was the one who had left her!*

"Just a minute!" she exclaimed, jumping up and crossing the room in a few quick strides. She grasped his arm and pulled. He turned with the movement of her hand, not resisting, and looked down into her face. "Tell me something. If you loved me so much, if you were so damn hurt, then why did you leave?"

"You know why. I explained it in my letter."

"What! You mean, leaving me because you loved me?" Isabelle asked sarcastically.

"Yes, dammit, that's what I mean!" he snapped back, his brows drawing together thunderously and his eyes shooting sparks. "It's what I said. I didn't lie. Although obviously you chose to believe what you wanted to."

"You don't leave someone because you love them!"

"You do if your love is going to hurt them. What was I supposed to do? Stay with you in Virginia and say goodbye to my career? Take you with me to New York? Good heavens, Isabelle, you were only eighteen years old. I already felt like a heel for getting involved with you, letting the situation get so out of hand. I was the one who was older, experienced. I knew better than to go out with you, let alone sleep with you. But having done it, I had to figure out how best to... to limit the damage."

"Limit the— You broke my heart!"

"You were eighteen. You'd never been in love before, never slept with a man. How could you really know whether you were in love with me or just infatuated?"

"You could have let me figure it out as we went along. That's the way most people do it."

"After I'd taken you away from college? Away from your family and friends, and brought you to a completely different world, a huge city where you knew nobody, where we'd be struggling to have enough to eat and a place to live? I was a poor actor who could barely earn enough to keep myself alive. How was I to support you? You don't know what it was like, living the way I did, hand to mouth, day to day, crashing in a friend's apartment when I had no place to live, eating one meal a day lots of times. That was no life for you. I could deal with it. I'd never had a lot of money. You'd grown up wealthy, the pampered only daughter of a country club family."

"So you just made the assumption that I couldn't take it? That I would fold?"

"I wasn't going to inflict it on you!" he shot back. "Sure, if I'd been selfish enough, I would have asked you to go to New York with me. I'd have let you endure that kind of life so I could have you. But even if I was enough of a heel to let you fall in love with me, I wasn't enough of one to put you in that kind of situation. To let you throw away your life so that I could make love to you for a few more months.''

''A few more months? There was a time limit on it?''

Michael grimaced. ''Be reasonable. It wouldn't have lasted. I had enough sense to know that. You would have, too, if you hadn't been a starry-eyed eighteen-year-old romantic.''

''Obviously you weren't.''

''You're right. I wasn't. I was five years older than that and I'd learned my lessons in a much harder school than you'd ever known. You were young and you were sheltered. You had no idea what awaited you. If you stayed there without me, I knew you'd go on to college like you had planned. You'd meet boys like yourself, a guy who could give you the kind of life you were used to. That's who you should have married. Not some actor from the wrong side of the tracks who couldn't offer you anything but poverty and uncertainty.''

Isabelle crossed her arms, regarding him coolly for a moment. ''So you decided I was better off without you. Tell me something, Michael. Are you a liar or just unbelievably arrogant?''

He looked at her blankly.

''Did it ever occur to you that I might have some interest in the matter? That I might want to help decide what to do with my future? I wanted to be an actor, too, you know. Why wouldn't I have thought that New York City was exactly where I wanted to be? Why do you assume that I was too weak to put up with a few hardships? It isn't as if I had no idea what an actor's life was like. I'd just spent several weeks with you and the other professional actors. I think I had a pretty good idea how you lived. And I knew that that was what I was facing when I got out of college and tried to find a job acting. I was ready to face it because I loved to act. Why wouldn't I have been ready to face it for the man I loved?''

"Hearing about it isn't the same as experiencing it."

"No. But you could have at least given me the chance. You didn't have to assume I was weak and shallow."

"I didn't think that of you."

"No? What else could you have thought of me? A woman who'd rather marry some guy with a nice car and 'prospects' than the man she loved? A woman too snobby to live in a crummy apartment, too fragile to cook or clean or get a job to help out with the expenses? Oh, that sounds like an admirable sort of person."

"That isn't what I thought of you. I just wanted to protect you, to keep you from making a serious mistake with your life. I wanted you to have a chance to see more of life before you tied yourself down to one person. I wanted you to have all the things a girl your age should have. Hell, Isabelle, I was thinking of you! I gave you up because I loved you!"

"Then God preserve me from your kind of love," Isabelle retorted bitterly. She turned and started away, then stopped and swung back around to say, "You didn't even have the nerve to tell me to my face. You could at least have done that, instead of leaving me a note."

"You weren't there. You were at your parents' house."

"You could have called. You could have come to see me. You didn't have to leave it in a note. But I can guess why you did. You were afraid to tell me face-to-face. You were a coward."

Michael shook his head, regret and frustration mingling in his face. "I tried to call you later, and you wouldn't talk to me."

"Did you honestly think I would? After what you'd done?"

He sighed. "I never meant to hurt you. I figured before long, after you'd gone to college and met someone else, you'd realize what a favor I'd done you. That you'd say, 'Thank heavens I didn't run away with that starving actor when I was eighteen.'"

"You say you loved me," Isabelle said coldly. "But you obviously didn't even know me."

Isabelle got through the rest of the day in an odd, numbed state; she felt almost as if she were sleepwalking, doing all the things she was supposed to, but without really feeling or thinking about any of it. She got in the open Jeep beside Michael, and they drove along the highway while the van drove in front, behind and beside it, taking shots. Then with the cameraman and the camera attached to the side of the car, they drove slowly over the same stretch of road while they took the close-up shots. Later the shots would be spliced together to be shown with music playing in the background.

When they were through, Isabelle rode back to the hotel in the van with the others, her eyes closed, pretending to sleep. She didn't want to talk to anyone, and when she reached the hotel she ordered her supper from room service and spent the remainder of the evening in the room by herself. She sat for a long time on the balcony, watching dusk settle over the ocean, remaining even after it was dark. The lights of a cruise ship anchored offshore twinkled in the distance, and the faint sounds of music from one of the party boats traveling over to the Isla Mujeres drifted across the water to her.

She thought about what Michael had told her, about the pain and sorrow she had seen in his face. *Had he re-*

ally loved her ten years ago? Had it hurt him to leave her? And had he truly left her because he thought it would be the best thing for her?

At first she rejected that idea. *How could anyone think that hurting someone he loved would be the best thing for her?* But Isabelle was honest enough to go past the wall of remembered pain and despair. She knew that if doctors had told her that Jenny had to attend a special school somewhere away from Isabelle, if they had said that that was the best way for her to learn and grow, then she would have agreed to send Jenny. She would have made Jenny go, even though it would have broken her heart to be separated from her... and even though it would have made Jenny sad at the time.

It was easy enough to see how someone would suppose that an eighteen-year-old was too young to make life decisions like giving up college and following the man she loved. Looking back, she could understand that someone else might think an eighteen-year-old girl's love was a passing, shallow fancy, that she really didn't know what love was. Michael would have assumed that her pampered life had left her ill prepared for living the hand-to-mouth existence of a penniless actor in New York; he would think she would be miserable, and he would be ashamed that he could not give her more. He had always been uneasy about the differences in their past: his childhood in a big, indifferent city, shuttled from foster home to foster home after his parents had died, and hers spent as the sheltered, beloved only child of well-to-do parents. She had ached for him then, when he talked about it, but she had thought that her love would heal all his wounds, would wear down the chip on his shoulder. But his preconceptions had taken him away from her before she had the chance to convince him.

With a groan, Isabelle buried her face in her hands. Long-buried hurt rose up in her, almost physically painful. She wanted to cry, but could not. Her emotions were a jumble of pain and regret and frustration. What a stupid, tangled mess it had been! *If she had only known how Michael had really felt, if he had only talked to her instead of leaving that damn note!*

She could have reasoned with him, convinced him that he was wrong. Then they would have been together when she found out she was pregnant with Jenny. He would have been with her when Jenny was born and would have supported her through all that worry and suffering.

With a sigh, Isabelle's hands fell away from her face and she leaned back in her chair. No, she realized, perhaps it would not have been better that way. If they had been together, if they had married and then Jenny had been born with all those problems, it would have made their lives very different. They wouldn't have had the money for the tremendous hospital and doctor bills. Michael would have been humiliated at taking money from her parents; he would have had to give up his acting career and get a regular, paying job. That would have been a hellish decision for him. His career had been all-important to him. After all, whatever his feelings for her had been, when his career had beckoned, he had not hesitated; he had gone. That was usually the way it was with actors. Acting was not just a profession to most, it was something that took over their lives, that was the very center of their beings. Nor would it have meant the end of only his dream. Isabelle doubted that she would have gone to California to pursue her career, either. *How could she have, if Michael had given up his career for her and the baby?*

And wouldn't the love they had shared have turned sour after a time? Wouldn't bitterness and recriminations have crept in? It was easy to say that life would have been better if they'd stayed together, but there was nothing to prove that would have been true; it might even have become worse.

Isabelle's thoughts left her feeling empty, as if an important part of her had been pulled out of herself. She supposed it had: she had lost the vision of her past that she always had before. It left her unsure of what she thought or felt.

She was still in a state of confusion the next morning when they began shooting. She felt awkward with Michael, and she avoided looking at him except when they were actually filming.

They shot the scenes of pursuit by the guerrilla fighters, using stunt doubles to film their crash into a ditch. After that, with Michael artistically decorated with a cut on his forehead and "blood" streaming down his face from the cut, they fled on foot. At a thatched-roof house, they found a bucket of water, and Jessica cleaned and bandaged Curtis's "wound." Curtis was confused and bewildered, and finally he asked her who she was. Gradually it dawned on Jessica that Curtis had lost his memory, at least temporarily.

Michael looked at her uncertainly and asked what they were to each other. Isabelle looked away, letting a crafty expression steal into her eyes, then turned back to him, smiling, and said, "Why, we're friends, Curtis. Very good friends."

There was the long, locked gaze so often used to end a scene in soaps, and then the scene was over.

"Great," Lyle said, pleased. "That's a wrap. Hey, kids, I'm happy to say that we are actually ahead of schedule. We have time to do the love scene this afternoon."

Seven

Isabelle was tired, and she had no desire to do a love scene now. Why, she could barely manage to look at Michael without feeling all jumbled-up inside. But it was "golden time," that wonderful late-afternoon time when the sun cast a special glow over everything, making it perfect for filming. She could hardly protest taking advantage of it, especially for a love scene.

They changed into their set of ragged, dirty clothes, and makeup artistically smudged their faces. First the cameras filmed the two of them coming upon the lovely lagoon and smiling with pure pleasure. Curtis jumped into the lagoon and urged Jessica in after him, finally reaching up and pulling her in. She spluttered and laughed, and they swam, teasing each other and laughing. Then they climbed out and stretched out on rocks beside the lagoon, letting the sun dry their clothing.

Next came the love scene. They rehearsed it first. Isabelle sat with her legs curled under her, on the edge of the flat rock, gazing down into the water. Michael, his shirt discarded, lay on his elbow on a flat rock a little behind and above her, watching her. Even though Isabelle's back was to him, she could feel his gaze moving over her body, and she swallowed, casting a glance back toward him.

His eyes went to the tear in her blouse that revealed the creamy skin of her shoulder, then down to where her blouse was tied beneath her breasts, showing her slim waist. His features softened sensually, and his eyes were lit with an inner fire.

"Tell me," he said huskily. "Before, when I can't remember, were we...just friends?"

Isabelle wet her lips nervously, letting her mouth open a bit, and her chest rise and fall more rapidly. It wasn't difficult to imitate the signs of passion; she was already growing warm just from his gaze. *Damn it, why did the man have to have such an effect upon her!*

What was harder was to put the hint of calculation in her eyes as she replied, "No...we were...more than friends."

He moved swiftly across the brief space that separated them. "How much more?" he asked, leaning forward until their faces were almost touching. His eyes burned into hers.

Isabelle wrenched her gaze away from him, half turning away. She choked out, "Close—we were close friends."

Michael knelt behind her and bent his head to kiss the patch of bare flesh exposed by the tear in her shirt. Isabelle's eyes fluttered closed and she let out a long sigh of pleasure. Michael's hands curled around her arms, holding her as his lips moved to her neck.

"This close?" he murmured huskily, kissing his way slowly up her throat.

"Yes," Isabelle moaned, her head lolling back against his shoulder. "Oh, yes."

"Jessica..." He pulled her around to face him, and his mouth came down on hers. Usually in rehearsals, kisses were not full kisses, but a mere indication of where and when they would kiss. This kiss, however, was full and deep, Michael's lips sinking relentlessly into hers. His breath came out in a rush against her cheek, his fingers bit into her arms, his mouth moved hungrily on hers.

Finally they pulled apart. Isabelle's cheeks were flushed, her eyes bright with passion. All around them the set was utterly still. They might have been alone together there. They gazed into each other's eyes for a moment, then slowly Isabelle lay down on her back, holding her arms up to Michael. He followed her, his mouth coming down to seize hers.

"Perfect." Lyle's voice cut through the silence, startling Michael and Isabelle. They came back to reality with a thud. Michael sat up abruptly. Color tinged the high ridge of his cheekbones, and his mouth was soft and sensually full.

Isabelle, too, sat up, realizing with chagrin how lost she had been to the world around them. She glanced over toward Lyle and the crew, then turned away, hunching her shoulders protectively. Michael reached down a hand to help her up, but she shook her head and rose without his assistance.

Isabelle left the rock and sat down on a bench, her arms wrapped around herself, while the crew scurried to check and recheck the cameras and light readings. She felt like a fool. She wondered if all the crew had been aware of how involved she had been in those kisses. They must have been, she knew, and she wondered how she would ever be able to look any of them in the eye again.

Then it was time for the shoot. Debbie and Callie retouched her hair and makeup, and Isabelle returned to her position, her stomach fluttering. Her lips could still feel the imprint of Michael's kisses. She sat down on the rock and closed her eyes, drawing in a calming breath and exhaling it slowly.

They began the scene again, this time with the cameras rolling. The sexual tension was even higher now. Isabelle could not help but remember the way the scene had progressed before and anticipate the touch of Michael's mouth again. When he moved over to her and gazed hotly into her eyes, the very air seemed to sizzle. He began to kiss her shoulder and neck, and fire seared down through Isabelle, melting her. She could hardly remember what she was supposed to do, but fortunately her part called for her to say nothing, only reveal her sensuous reaction to Michael's kisses.

That was easy. With every brush of his lips against her skin, another shiver shook her, and by the time he kissed her, her entire body was taut and quivering. Michael's mouth pressed into hers. His kiss was hotter, harder, deeper than before. His tongue came into her mouth, velvety, hungry, demanding. Isabelle responded, her tongue twining with his in a passionate dance. He groaned and clasped her even more tightly against him.

They forgot to pull apart and look at one another before Isabelle lay down, inviting him into her arms. Instead, they eased back onto the ground instinctively, arms still locked around one another.

"Cut! Okay, cut!" It took two calls for Lyle's voice to register with them.

Michael's mouth left hers reluctantly, and he sat up. Isabelle felt utterly boneless; she thought she might have to lie right there forever. She ran her tongue over her damp, kiss-softened lips, and Michael's eyes darkened with passion. He cleared his throat and looked away, shoving his hands back into his hair.

"You forgot to break," Lyle pointed out.

"What?" Michael turned to look at the director, his expression dazed.

"The break," Lyle said, suppressing a smile. "Right at the end. You break the kiss and Isabelle lies down, reaches toward you."

"Oh. Yeah. Sorry."

Isabelle couldn't imagine why the scene wouldn't be fine the way they had done it. It seemed a rather minor point, and God knows this take must be good enough to print. However, she merely nodded, unable to pull together her woolly thoughts enough to argue.

Michael moved back to his rock, and they played the scene again. His eyes were blazing with sensual heat as he spoke to her, and his voice was gravelly with desire. Tendrils of fire darted through Isabelle's abdomen at the sound of it, and when he kissed her bare shoulder and throat, she shivered with passion, unaware of how her face softened sensually. She was eager for his kiss now; it was all she could do to hold back until his mouth came down on hers. When at last it did, a little groan escaped her throat.

The sound almost undid Michael. He shuddered, and his mouth ground into hers, his tongue filling her mouth with heat. His hands dug into her hair, as if holding her head still to the depredation of his lips. Isabelle felt as if she were consumed with flames. Her hands skimmed over his shoulders and back, caressing his bare skin.

Finally he broke their kiss and pulled back. He gazed at her, his chest heaving. Isabelle stared back at him, her lips soft and swollen from his ruthless kisses, her eyes lambent with desire. She did not hear the sucked-in breath of the cameraman as he zoomed in for a close-up of her face. She was too caught up in desire, her whole body thrumming for Michael's touch.

Isabelle lay down on her back, her dark hair rippling over the rock and cascading off it. Her eyes never left Michael's. Then she raised her arms, silently inviting him to come to her, and he came down to kiss her again.

The director called "Cut," and there were audible sighs from all the crew. Michael drew back reluctantly.

"That was perfect. Loved the way your hair fell over the rock and off it, Isabelle. Remember to keep her right there, Cassie. Okay, let's take a break. Then we'll rehearse the next scene."

Isabelle nodded, unable to meet anyone's eyes. Now that the scene was over, she was aware of how sensual it had been. She had heard the soft noises from the crew when the scene ended, the whispered comments. Anything that could stir a jaded television crew like that had to have been exceedingly stirring. It made her hot with embarrassment to think how she had revealed herself. There was no way any of them would think she was just acting.

She moved away from the lagoon, ignoring everyone. But she was very aware, nonetheless, of where Michael went. Cassie Shumway brought her a soft drink, and Isabelle sat down on the bench, pretending to study her script while she drank the cola. Looking down at her front, she could see the outline of her hardened nipples pushing against the formfitting cotton top. She blushed, fighting down an urge to cover her breasts, knowing that the gesture would only make her condition more obvious.

However, she could not keep from glancing up and over at the low rock wall, where Michael sat, one foot up on the wall and his arm braced on that leg. He was watching her; she saw his gaze drop to the front of her shirt. She blushed fiery red and dropped her eyes back to her script.

No doubt he was enjoying her discomfiture, she thought furiously. She hated the way she had reacted to him. Even if he hadn't been the villain she had always assumed he was, it seemed incredibly weak of her to just melt at his kiss like that. After all, it wasn't as if she still loved him. No, it was simply animal desire, and Isabelle disliked letting her control slip, especially in front of all these people. She could just imagine the kind of comments she would have to endure from some of them for the next few days.

"All right, kids," Lyle announced, clapping his hands to get everyone's attention. "Let's get back to work. We have to move quickly to keep this light."

Isabelle moved back to her spot reluctantly, fearing the passion that could come sweeping back up in her. Yet she could not deny that deep inside she was also eagerly awaiting Michael's kiss, her hunger rising up. She wanted to feel his lips on hers again, wanted to be seared with his heat.

Debbie darted in, arranging Isabelle's hair so that it rippled smoothly over the rocks again. Michael lay down beside her, and Isabelle's breath quickened at his nearness. He leaned across her, planting one arm on the other side of her as it had been in the scene before. His face loomed over her, still marked with the slackness of desire. Heat blossomed between Isabelle's legs at this evidence that he had been as moved by their previous scene as she had been.

They rehearsed the scene, talking their way through the kisses and caresses, making sure that they were as mechanical and brief as they normally were during rehearsal. It was impossible for Isabelle to be entirely indifferent to his fingers skimming down her arm and her side or his lips brushing against hers; she felt an inner quiver each time. But she was sure that it was nothing that was visible to anyone else, even Michael.

When it was time to film, Isabelle slid her arms around his neck, and Michael lowered his face to hers, his mouth covering hers. Isabelle heard Lyle calling for the cameras to roll, but it didn't matter. Michael's mouth was already moving against hers. She struggled mentally for a time, trying to retain her control over the scene, to kiss him in the same detached way she had enacted other love scenes. But heat was flooding through her body, and her mind was quickly losing all thought of anything except how hot and firm his lips were and how much she wanted to feel his tongue in her mouth again. Michael deepened his kiss, as if he knew what she wanted. Or perhaps it was simply that he wanted the same thing. His tongue explored her mouth, tasting again all its remembered sweetness. They kissed again and again, the barely cooled embers of their passion flaring into life. Heat pooled between Isabelle's legs, and she ached to wrap them around Michael, to press that hot seat of her desire against him. His hands clenched in her hair, and he groaned.

Pulling his mouth from hers, he began to rain kisses down her throat, and his hand slid down her side and onto the naked flesh of her stomach, bared by the blouse knotted beneath her breasts. Isabelle quivered when he touched the sensitive skin, and she let out a choked moan. His mouth came back to hers, and they strained together, kissing passionately.

When the director called, "Cut," it was a long moment before Michael pulled back. Isabelle gazed up at him. His face was flushed, and the skin seemed stretched too tightly across his facial bones. His breath was coming fast, and when he looked down at her, his eyes were so hot that she felt almost as if they seared her skin. Isabelle had the awful feeling that her face reflected her desire just as clearly; she dared not look over at the director and crew.

"Sorry, people," Lyle was saying. "A bird flew past you during that scene, ruined the take. We'll have to do another one."

Isabelle saw the muscles jump in Michael's jaw, and he closed his eyes for a moment before he let out his breath in a long sigh.

"Okay," he said briefly and turned back to the position in which they had started.

The heat of his body enveloped her. Isabelle had the awful feeling that she might lose control during this scene and start moaning and whimpering or moving her hands over him in a manner unsuitable for television. Looking up into his glittering eyes, it occurred to Isabelle that they might simply explode into lovemaking in front of the whole crew. She let out a shaky breath.

"Please . . ." she whispered.

Michael groaned and sank his lips into hers. Isabelle went up in flames. She clung to Michael, working her mouth against his as they kissed again and again. His hands moved restlessly—in her hair, down her arm, along her hip. She could feel his hard desire against her leg, and a throbbing ache came between her legs.

He threw his leg across hers, pressing her intimately against that hard length. Isabelle sank her hands into his hair. His hand caressed her side; his thumb brushed against the swell of her breast. Michael tore his lips from hers and kissed her face and neck, his breath rasping in his throat. His mouth moved downward, pausing to lave the delicate hollow of her throat, then drifting ever lower toward the swell of her breast.

Isabelle's breasts rose, aching to feel his touch; her nipples tightened into hard buds, pushing eagerly against her shirt. She wanted to feel him against her naked skin, to have his fingers on her breasts, to open her legs and take him into her.

It took three calls before the director's voice finally cut through the haze of their passion. Dazedly, Michael lifted his head and looked up.

"Sorry," Lyle said. "You know we can't have your body on hers from the waist down, Michael."

Michael glanced down and realized that he was indeed stretched out full-length on top of Isabelle. Hastily he moved to the side, mumbling, "I'm sorry."

Isabelle, coming to her senses, realized what a scene they must have presented to everyone present, and she blushed fiery red.

"We'll have to shoot it over," Lyle went on.

"What?" Michael's voice came out as a croak. He stared at the director. His face was stamped with passion, his eyes heavy-lidded and fogged with desire, his mouth full and wide, his skin flushed. He sat up, letting out an expletive, and shoved a hand through his hair.

The director's lips quivered, and he hastily covered his mouth with his hand. Someone snickered and quickly muffled it. Michael's eyes narrowed, and he looked around at the crew. One of the men turned away, and another bit his lip, widening his eyes innocently.

"Wait a minute!" Michael exclaimed. "This is a joke, isn't it? You got it on the first take. Last time, too!"

One of the cameramen burst out laughing, and everyone joined in. Lyle guffawed, holding on to his sides. Michael groaned and fell back onto the ground. He began to curse fluently.

"A joke?" Isabelle sat up, fury flooding through her. "You mean this is one of your stupid practical jokes? Making us do all those takes?"

It didn't surprise her. The crew and actors often engaged in practical jokes, a practice born, no doubt, of the long hours of tedium between takes, as well as the familiarity of constantly working together. Isabelle had more than once helped to further one or another of the jokes, and she herself had been caught twice. The other times she had laughed along with the others, but at the moment she was having trouble seeing the humor in the situation. Her entire body was thrumming with unsatisfied desire. Worse than that, the hunger Michael could create in her had been so obvious to everyone that they had built a practical joke on it.

Without thinking, she jumped to her feet and lithely clambered up from the rocks and across the path to where Lyle stood, watching her somewhat apprehensively. Beside him was a picnic table, on which the crew had piled various pieces of equipment. The cooler, from which they had been pulling soft drinks all day to quench their thirst, was also there. Isabelle veered slightly to her left, picked up the cooler, now empty except for a little ice and the water that had melted in it all day, and turned to the director. Lyle's eyes widened, and he started to move, but he wasn't fast enough. Isabelle hurled the cold water upon him, tossed the cooler aside and stalked off. Behind her, she could hear Michael's roar of laughter.

Isabelle's satisfaction was short-lived. She jumped in one of the ubiquitous taxis waiting outside the lagoon's entrance, having no desire to return with all the others in the vans. On the long ride home, her anger cooled, and she regretted her display of temper. It hadn't helped; the others still were aware of her passionate response to Michael, perhaps even more so since she'd gotten so angry over the joke. She was still just as embarrassed, and now she would have to apologize to Lyle, as well.

Feeling thoroughly disgruntled, she went immediately to her room to shower away the dirt, grit and sunblock. Then, wrapped in her terry-cloth bathrobe, she ordered dinner from room service and sat on the balcony to eat it, watching the darkness gather on the ocean. She set the tray on the small table to the side of the chair and just sat, watching the stars and the lights on the water and wishing that she could relax.

Despite the shower and rest, she was keyed up. It was ten o'clock, and they had an early shoot tomorrow; she ought to get to bed. But Isabelle knew that any attempt to sleep right now would be useless. The heat had died down in her body, but there was still an unsatisfied, achy feeling low in her abdomen, and her nerves were as taut and twanging as violin strings. She could not stop thinking about Michael, could not keep from remembering the way he had kissed her this afternoon.

With a low growl of frustration, she stood up from her chair and stalked to the railing. She stood there, looking out at the ocean, her hands curled around the metal railing. There was the sound of a sliding glass door opening

on the balcony next to her, and she whirled around, startled.

Michael stepped out of his door and softly pulled it
closed. "Hello, Isabelle."

Isabelle grimaced. *This was the last thing she needed—
to have to talk to Michael.* "Hello."

Her voice was notably lacking in enthusiasm, but Michael didn't seem to notice. He came to the waist-high
metal railing between their balconies and rested his hands
on the top of it. Neither of them had turned on the lights
on their balconies, and curtains shaded the light from
inside their rooms, but there was enough moonlight to
enable Isabelle to see him. The cool light washed over his
face, highlighting the strong cheekbones and turning the
blue eyes dark. He was wearing shorts and a tank top,
and the bare expanse of his skin gleamed. Just seeing him
made her nerves begin to hum.

Michael smiled. "I liked the way you handled Lyle today."

"Oh." Isabelle shook her head. "I shouldn't have done
that. I'll have to apologize to him."

"Nonsense. He deserved it. They all did. They
shouldn't have involved you in the joke. It was me Lyle
was trying to get—retaliation for that one I pulled on him
two weeks ago. I should have guessed. They should have
told you, but..." He shrugged. "I think it was a spur-of-
the-moment thing. They saw how kissing you affected
me. It was too good a joke to pass up."

Isabelle, too, moved up to the railing. She shouldn't
stand this close to him, she knew, but she could not seem
to control her limbs any more than she had been able to
control herself this afternoon. She stood there, not quite
daring to look Michael in the eyes, but instead concen-

trating her gaze on the railing, where her fingernails idly picked at a flake of peeling paint.

Michael's hands came down to grip the railing on either side of her hand. Heat rose in Isabelle, and her breath was suddenly shorter.

"I guess I'm lucky it didn't turn out any worse," he said huskily. "There were a few moments this afternoon when I hardly knew where I was, I was so crazy for you."

He moved forward until he was pressed against the railing, his body only inches from hers. His breath ruffled Isabelle's hair, and she could smell the faintly soapy scent of his body. He put his hands on her shoulders, and a shiver ran down through her. She told herself that she should move away, but she could not.

Slowly he smoothed his hands down her arms, and even though the thick terry-cloth material lay between their skins, Isabelle still trembled at his touch. Unconsciously, she swayed toward him, leaning against the railing.

"I wanted to touch you," he told her thickly, nuzzling her hair. "I wanted to peel off your clothes and look at you. Caress you. Kiss you."

His hands moved to her hips and crept back up her body, lingering over the full mounds of her breasts. Isabelle's breath turned ragged, and she leaned her head against his chest, too weak to move, too hungry for his touch. It was what she, too, had yearned for this afternoon. Her breasts swelled and ached, remembering the glory of his fingers on them. Her nipples were hard and thrusting.

"I can't get my mind off you," Michael went on in that low, mesmerizing voice. "I've been hard as a rock all evening, just thinking about you."

Isabelle drew in a shaky breath and looked up at him. Just his words were enough to melt her loins. Gazing into his face—the hot, hungry eyes, the taut expression of desire—she was flooded with such heat that she thought her legs might buckle beneath her.

Michael's hands moved up to the bare triangle of skin that showed above her robe. "Do you have anything on beneath that robe?"

She shook her head mutely, very aware of the fact that only the tied belt at the waist kept her robe closed. Michael spread his fingers across her chest, his fingers sliding beneath the edges of the material. Slowly he moved downward, shoving the heavy cloth aside. His hands slid over her breasts, opening the top of her robe. He stood for a moment, gazing at her bared breasts.

His face was heavy and dark with passion as his eyes moved hungrily over her breasts. "You're just as beautiful as I remembered," he told her hoarsely. "Maybe even more so. Oh, Isabelle..."

He yanked the sides of the robe apart, and the loosely tied belt came undone, revealing all of her naked body to his sight.

Eight

Michael sucked in his breath. His gaze moved slowly down over her body. Isabelle closed her eyes and gripped the railing tightly. Hot moisture pooled between her legs, and her knees felt as if they might give way if she didn't cling to some support. She loved feeling Michael's searing gaze on her; with every fiber of her being, she ached for him to touch her.

He reached out and lightly trailed his hands over her breasts, sending hundreds of shivers tingling through her. His thumbs circled the points of her nipples, making them tighten. He traced the larger aureoles around the hardened buds and gently cupped her breasts in his palms.

"So beautiful," he murmured. "So soft."

His hands slid down from her breasts onto her narrow waist, then brushed across the thrusting pelvic bones and delved beneath her robe, roaming back over her hips and caressing the curve of her buttocks. His fingertips dug into the soft flesh, and a shudder shook him.

He bent and pressed his lips to the soft curve of her breast, trailing down over the trembling globe until he found the small fleshy mound of her nipple. His lips teased the bud, brushing it, kissing it, nibbling at it with teeth sheathed by his lips, and all the while his hands moved over her hips and buttocks, stretching down to caress her thighs.

Isabelle whimpered and pressed closer to him, the metal railing digging into the soft flesh of her stomach. Michael made a noise deep in his throat and hungrily took her nipple into his mouth. He suckled, caressing the hard button with his tongue, and his hand curved around her buttock and between her legs from behind. He groaned at the moisture he found there, evidence of Isabelle's pulsing desire, and his fingers explored the wet, satiny flesh. Isabelle gasped, and her hands went to his shoulders, caressing him frantically. His hands and mouth were driving her wild, vaulting her long-suppressed desire to a fever pitch.

"Michael," she murmured, trailing kisses over his arm and shoulders, shoving aside the material of his tank top to reach more of his skin. "Oh, Michael, Michael, please..."

Michael groaned at the sound of her plea and straightened. His hands went to either side of her head, plunging deep into her hair, and his mouth found hers. He kissed her deeply, his tongue filling her mouth. Her breasts pressed into his chest, but it wasn't enough for him. He ached to feel Isabelle against the length of him, to move between her legs and feel her legs wrap around him. The metal bars of the railing frustrated him, and he swung his leg over the railing, blindly climbing over without breaking off their kiss.

His foot struck the small table in the corner of Isabelle's balcony, sending the room service tray with all its dishes crashing onto the cement floor. The clatter was horrendous. Michael froze, still astride the railing with one foot on Isabelle's balcony floor. Belatedly he released her and looked down at the mess of broken crockery. Isabelle stepped back, bumping into her chair and knocking over the large vase behind it. It fell with a thump, breaking the lip, and rattled noisily across the balcony to the other side, where it banged against the opposite metal railing.

"What the hell is going on over there?" Three balconies away, someone stood up, turning toward them. It was the day player who had come with them to portray the leader of the guerrillas chasing them. He had obviously been sitting on his balcony, enjoying the evening and the drink in his hand until the noise of the crashing tray had disrupted the quiet night air.

Isabelle's eyes widened in horror, and she hastily wrapped her robe around herself. At that moment, the sliding glass door on the other side of her room opened and Lyle stepped out, looking curiously over at them.

All up and down the row of rooms, heads were popping out of the balcony doors to see what had occasioned the crash. Most of them were members of their crew.

Isabelle blushed to the roots of her hair. It had to be obvious what she and Michael had been doing, especially with her clutching her robe together and him perched on the railing between their balconies, half on and half off.

She let out a groan of embarrassment and fled back into her room, slamming the patio door shut and locking it behind her, leaving Michael alone on the balcony, cursing inventively.

Isabelle had never been so embarrassed in her life. Everyone on the crew was bound to know what she had been doing on the balcony with Michael, especially after those sizzling scenes they'd filmed by the lagoon that afternoon. And, of course, none of them would keep their mouths shut about it, which meant that as soon as they returned to L.A., everyone connected with the show would know that she had melted like wax in Michael's arms.

She lay on her bed for hours, grinding her teeth in anger and frustration. Her phone rang persistently for thirty minutes. She hadn't answered it, sure that it was either Michael or one of the women on location with them, wanting to know all the details of what had happened. Finally, she took it off the hook and stuffed the receiver under a pillow.

Isabelle stared at the ceiling, wondering how she could get through the next day of shooting when she couldn't bear to see any of the others. She also wondered how she was going to get through this night. There wasn't any place on her body, she thought, that didn't ache or throb or tingle with desire. She knew it would be long, tormented hours before her body cooled down enough to let her go to sleep. *And how in the world was she going to stay out of Michael's bed?*

The next morning when she went down to join the others in the lobby, she was red-eyed and leaden-lidded from lack of sleep. She ignored the sly smile Debbie cast in her direction, as well as the curious glances from the rest of the crew, and marched up to Lyle, shoulders squared, to apologize for dumping water over him the day before.

He smiled at her a little shamefacedly. "It's all right. I deserved it. I shouldn't have done that without warning you. Michael raked me over the coals yesterday for letting you get caught, too, when I was paying him back." He shrugged. "I didn't know that you two were . . . well, you know, that there was anything going on between you."

"There's not," Isabelle retorted flatly. She made herself smile to take the sting from her abrupt words. She liked Lyle, and she didn't want to be at odds with the director. "I don't know how we ever get any work done, the way you guys are about jokes."

"Livens up the day," Lyle responded jovially, just as eager as she to get rid of the strain between him and one of the show's stars.

Isabelle turned and caught sight of Michael, just entering the lobby. He looked as if he'd gotten as little sleep as she had. Quickly she turned and hurried outside to the waiting vans. She climbed into the front passenger seat, knowing that there, at least, Michael would be unable to sit beside her, and settled down to wait for the others.

When the rest of them came out, Michael got into the back of the van. Isabelle could feel him watching her, but she refused to even glance back at him. Once they arrived at the location, she went straight to Debbie and Callie for makeup and wardrobe. Then she moved away while Michael was getting his makeup done and sat down on a large rock, studying her script intently.

After he was finished in Makeup, Michael started toward her. Isabelle pretended to be immersed in her script, hoping that he would take the hint and go away. She

ought desperately of dodging into the women's bathroom, but she knew how foolish that would look to everyone else. *Why couldn't the man just take the hint and
leave her alone?*

Michael stopped in front of her, only inches away. Is-
belle continued to pretend to read. He waited, folding
his arms and assuming an air of great patience.

"Oh, stop," Isabelle snapped finally, looking up at
him. "Why won't you go away? I don't want to talk to
you."

"I want to talk to you."

Isabelle sighed. "We have nothing to say."

"Really?" His voice was heavy with sarcasm. "I would
have thought we had a great deal to say. You obviously
have some very strong feelings."

"You're right. I very strongly would like not to have to
talk to you."

"Why? Isabelle . . . look, I'm sorry I created a distur-
bance last night. I'm not usually that clumsy. I know you
were embarrassed that everyone saw we were out on the
balcony."

"They saw a good bit more than that. It was obvious
what we'd been doing. I was practically undressed, and
you—"

"I know, I know. I was crawling over the wall like a
seventeen-year-old in heat." Michael grimaced. "I'm
sorry. Believe me, the last thing I intended was to embarrass you and bring everyone out on their balconies to
see us."

"It wasn't your fault any more than it was mine. It
was . . . just a mistake."

"No," he whispered, so fiercely that Isabelle looked up
at him in surprise. "Don't say that. It wasn't a mistake.

It was exactly right. And it was inevitable. We've been heading straight toward it ever since I joined the show.''

Isabelle shook her head vehemently. "No."

"We can't ignore what we feel for each other," he protested. "At least, I can't. It was never finished between us. That was my fault. You were right when you told me that I left before you came back because I was a coward. I was. I was scared that if I told you face-to-face, you'd try to argue me out of it. And I was afraid I wouldn't be able to follow through. I wanted you so much, loved you so much, I was scared I'd give in to whatever you wanted, even if I knew it was wrong. So I ran. I was wrong. All those years it's still been there inside us, dormant. But never closed."

"Then let's close it now. I'll tell you that I no longer hate you for it. You did what you thought was best, and maybe it was. I don't know. We certainly wouldn't be where we are now if we had stayed together. But that was years ago. We're different people now. I'm not eighteen anymore, and I'm not interested in a giddy teenage romance. I like my life the way it is. I don't want any disturbances."

"What, you're twenty-eight now and an old woman? Give me a break, Isabelle. What's wrong with a little giddiness? What's wrong with romance? Maybe we are different people now, and maybe it won't be the same with us. But where's the harm in seeing? What would be so wrong about taking a chance?"

"You can't see the harm?" Frantically, Isabelle scrambled to come up with some reason that did not involve Jenny. "For one thing, there's the show. I never get involved with anyone I work with. I hate the gossip. A soap set is like a small town. You know that. Everyone in the whole cast and crew will be gossiping about us. We've already given them a week's worth of gossip since yesterday. And what happens when the affair turns sour? We still have to work together."

"Oh, and it's so easy working together now," Michael mocked. "It's such a breeze being in this state of sexual limbo with each other."

"It would be even worse if we hated each other or if one of us grew indifferent and the other was madly in love. It would be an impossible working situation."

"It seems pretty impossible to me right now."

"Michael, please...."

"Come on, Iz. I don't get it. I understand it's difficult to have an affair with someone on the same show. It could be very awkward, worse than awkward. But there's nothing we can do about it now. We are already involved. We can't stop that."

"We can, and we will!" Isabelle insisted.

"Why? And don't give me this garbage about the show. Why are you so damn scared?"

Isabelle sprang to her feet. "Can't you leave it alone? Hasn't anyone ever turned you down before? I don't want to have an affair with you! Just stay away from me!"

She realized belatedly that their voices had been growing louder and louder, until she had practically shouted her last words. Everyone on the set had stopped whatever they were doing and were watching them avidly. Isabelle groaned.

"Well, that will certainly make all the gossip die down," Michael commented dryly.

Isabelle glared at him. He raised his hands, palms out, as if in surrender.

"All right. I give up. Obviously you're not willing to talk about whatever's bothering you. I can't make you give us a chance.'' His lips tightened, and he dropped his hands to his side. ''Let's just get back to work.''

He turned on his heel and walked away. Isabelle swallowed hard and followed him.

They finished shooting the following day. Michael and Isabelle avoided each other as much as possible. Isabelle could see that this was causing just as much gossip among the crew as the incident on the balcony had. It was a distinct relief when they flew back to L.A.

Or course, the location crew and director told everyone what had happened in Cancún, so the gossip about the two of them spread like wildfire throughout the rest of the staff and cast. Everyone from Felice to Amanda, the head of Wardrobe, hinted to Isabelle that they were ready and willing to let Isabelle unburden her heart to them about the matter. Isabelle laughed and shrugged it off as best she could, saying with a lightness that even she could tell rang false, that nothing was ''going on'' between Michael and her.

That was, of course, the literal truth. But there was another truth, as well, and that was that, no matter how much Isabelle avoided being around Michael, she could not stop thinking about him. Whether she was on the set, rehearsing or filming a scene with him, or at home alone with Jenny, her mind circled relentlessly around him. She remembered that evening on the balcony and the feel of his arms around her, his body hot and urgent against hers, his mouth consuming her.

Over the years, she had held herself aloof from sexual entanglements. Listening to other women talk about their feelings for one man or another, she had congratulated herself a little smugly that her head always kept a firm rule over her senses and emotions. Her experience with

Michael years ago had taught her not to get carried away, she thought. Now she wondered if it was simply that Michael was the only man who had ever really put her control to the test. Perhaps it hadn't been intelligence or self-control that kept her life on an even keel, but simply the absence of the one man who really stirred her passions. It was a lowering thought.

However, Isabelle was determined not to give in. She was *not* opening herself up again to the dangers of falling in love with Michael Traynor. Her heart was still whole and hers, and she was determined not to let him into it. She maintained her cool, remote attitude toward him on the set, staying in her dressing room as much as possible and leaving immediately after work so that she would have to be around him as little as possible.

But after only a week, she was beginning to wonder how long she was going to be able to keep this up. It was getting harder and harder to stay away from Michael. Sometimes when she happened to glance over at him on the set, she caught a glimpse of something in his eyes that made her feel weak all over. She had the awful feeling that if he ever decided to actively pursue her, she was all too likely to topple from her pedestal of self-control.

Michael stared moodily into his almost-empty coffee cup. He didn't know how much longer he could take this. Every day since they had returned from Mexico had been a hell of unremitting tension. The nights had been even worse. He wanted Isabelle, wanted to take her into his bed and make love to her for long, slow hours. He didn't think anything else would stop the ache inside him, but he was also beginning to think that that would never happen.

He had to see Isabelle every day on the set, had to hear her voice, had to watch as she talked and laughed with other people in a free-and-easy manner that she never displayed to him. Though they had shot no love scenes since they returned from Cancún, many of his scenes with Isabelle were building up to the climactic moment when they would make love. There was a gradual building of sexual tension both in their dialogue and in their actions. They accidentally touched; they looked at each other with longing; they moved close, then pulled away in the intricate mating ritual of a soap opera love affair.

The stiffness between Michael and Isabelle, the underlying tension, charged their scenes with electricity. They could not speak or move without betraying a taut awareness of each other, lending an air of such realism to their scenes that the tapes fairly crackled.

It was not hard for Michael to play the scenes; the far more difficult acting was to pretend after the scene was over that he and Isabelle were nothing but two professionals doing a job, that he was as indifferent to her as she appeared to be to him.

On the set and off, it seemed as if he could think of nothing but Isabelle. He remembered the way it had felt to touch her skin, to feel her mouth yield under his. He thought about the way her breasts had fit into his palms, deliciously heavy and soft, the nipples prickling under his thumbs. Whenever he looked at her at the studio, he found himself mentally stripping her, his body turning hot and hard with desire. Yet it was no better when he was alone in his apartment at night, for then he thought of that night on her balcony and how beautiful she had been when he parted the sides of her robe and looked at her naked body. Sometimes it was hours before he could manage to go to sleep, and then he would awaken the next morning bleary-eyed and still taut with unspent passion.

Worst of all, they were working up to the big scene in the cave, where Curtis and Jessica would make love. That was something Michael wasn't sure he could endure. The love scenes before had been bad enough, but these would be longer and more intense—and he was already so wired up that Michael thought he might explode if he so much as kissed her.

He didn't know how he was going to get through it. Yet there was no way that he could get out of it. The entire filming for the past two weeks had been moving toward this point. The sweeps had already started, and next week, the first of the Cancún episodes would air.

Michael sighed and drained the dregs of his coffee, then crumpled up the cup and tossed it into the trash can. He opened the door of his dressing room and started out into the hall. He stopped short when he saw Isabelle standing at the other end of the hall, talking to Carol Nieman. For a moment he stood, watching Isabelle undetected. Isabelle's hair was down, the sophisticated hairdo she wore on the set brushed out. Her face had been scrubbed clean of makeup, and she wore sandals, a cropped T-shirt and cutoffs. She looked as different from her character on the show as she could be—and she looked even sexier to Michael.

His hands itched to glide over the soft skin of her cheeks. He wanted to shove his fingers into her thick dark hair, to lay his head against hers and breathe in her unique scent, to slide his hands over her firm, lithe body.

Carol turned and caught sight of him and smiled hugely. "Michael!" She held out one hand to him. "You're still here, too. I'm so glad. I was afraid everyone had left."

"Isabelle and I had the last scene today," Michael said, going down the hall to join them.

Isabelle turned to look at him, but without Carol's joyous smile. It was the same indifferent, almost blank, look with which she always regarded him these days, a look that infuriated Michael even as it cut him, a look that made him long to grab her arms and shake her—or kiss her until she melted against him as she had last week in Cancún.

"I was just telling Isabelle how well the new story line is doing. We're getting lots of mail. Everyone can sense that you two are going to be an item, and we haven't even shown the first of the Cancún shows yet! Danny is so pleased. He's seen some of the advances from Cancún, and he thinks they look marvelous."

Carol hugged Michael enthusiastically, then turned in her usual quick way. "Well, I have to run now. I'm doing a meeting upstairs with the writers in two minutes. I just wanted to tell you how pleased we are with both of you."

"Remember that at contract time," Michael joked, and Carol shook an admonishing finger at him.

Then she was off down the hall to the stairs, her heels clacking busily on the tiled floor. Michael turned toward Isabelle. The long, wide hall was empty except for them. He suspected that all the rooms were empty, too. The crew had no doubt left immediately after the filming; only he and Isabelle had stayed to remove their costumes and makeup.

"You leaving?" he asked casually, trying to match her air of calm unconcern.

"Yes." Isabelle started toward the exit at the opposite end of the hall, and Michael fell in beside her.

"I'll walk you out, then," he said.

They strode along for a moment in silence. Michael desperately wracked his brain for something—anything!—to say. He could smell the trace of Isabelle's perfume, mingled with the scent of the cream she used to remove her makeup, and it sent tendrils of desire curling through his abdomen. He remembered when he had first known her ten years ago and he would wait for her after rehearsal or a performance and walk her back to the Victorian rooming house where she lived with other students.

"Remember the porch at your rooming house?" he asked suddenly.

Isabelle glanced at him, eyes widening with surprise. Emotions quivered through her. She had been careful to keep all her defenses up around Michael since that night on the balcony, but now, somehow, with this reminder of the past, he had managed to sneak in around her walls. She remembered the wide covered porch with its narrow columns and gingerbread trim. They had sat in wooden Adirondack deck chairs, holding hands—or sometimes cuddled together in one of the wider chairs, her head on his shoulder—and talked. Isabelle could feel the heavy humid air of the hot summer nights, could even smell the heady scent of the roses climbing up the trellis at one end of the porch.

"Yes," she replied in a low voice. "I remember."

"And the hamburgers at Bobby's?"

Isabelle chuckled, her throat clogging inexplicably with tears. "Yes, and the hot cherry pies at the City Café."

"Oh, God, yes." Michael stopped, taking her hands in his and turning her to face him. "Most of all, I remember you. Isabelle, please...don't shut me out. Give me a chance. Give us a chance."

Isabelle stood, gazing at him, her heart pounding faster. He had taken her by surprise. When he started to reminisce, she had let down her guard and joined in. Now she was having a hard time pulling her defenses back together. It was too difficult to think with Michael this close to her.

Sensing that she was wavering, Michael brought her hands up to his lips and kissed each one, slowly and gently, his mouth lingering, his breath teasing her flesh.

"I haven't been able to think of anything but you for a week. Longer than that. I've wanted you from the day I walked into the studio and saw you again. Maybe even before that." He closed his eyes, sensuously rubbing one of her palms across his cheek.

Isabelle's legs turned to putty. She knew she could not walk away; she was afraid she might sink to the floor right there. The fire she had done her best all week to tamp down suddenly sprang into life again in her abdomen.

"Every day I watch you," Michael went on huskily. "And I wonder how I'm ever going to do that scene Monday without losing control."

His words sent electric shivers through her. Isabelle unconsciously swayed toward him. He gave a little tug, just enough to pull her the rest of the way to his chest. His arms went around her. Michael leaned back against the wall, holding Isabelle pressed against his body all the way up and down. His hands slid up to her shoulders and down over her back, sliding underneath the waistband of her loose-fitting shorts and over her buttocks. His fingers dug in, lifting her up and more firmly into him, rubbing her pelvis against his.

"I like you like this," he murmured. "All scrubbed and clean."

"Plain, you mean." Isabelle struggled to keep the breathlessness she felt out of her voice. She could not bring herself to move away, to leave the excitement of his body. She felt as if she were lost, swirling ever downward in a spiral of desire. She couldn't help herself; she wasn't even sure she wanted to.

"Plainly beautiful." He nuzzled into her hair, breathing in her seductive scent. "If all women looked the way you do now, all the cosmetics firms would go bankrupt. Isabelle . . . say you still want me."

"You must know I do," she replied shakily. It was wonderful to stand this way, her body flush against his, to feel his fingers upon her skin and his body quickening with passion beneath hers.

"You can hide it more easily than I," he retorted.

Isabelle's husky laugh sent shivers down his spine. His hand swept up between them and cupped one of her breasts, squeezing gently.

Isabelle drew in a sharp breath and whispered, "Not easily enough." She knew she should tell him to stop, to let her go, but she could not say the words.

"Make love with me," he murmured.

"And what will happen after that?"

"Whatever you want."

Isabelle shook her head in a last feeble attempt to stop what was happening. "It doesn't work that way."

"It can. It will." He tilted up her chin and bent down to kiss her.

His lips were firm and warm, working magic upon her. Isabelle went up on tiptoe and wrapped her arms around his neck, giving herself up to his kiss. For this moment, it was easy to believe in love. To believe in forever. Isabelle could not remember all the reasons why she should not give in to Michael's kisses. Rationality and sanity fled before the storm of desire rising up in her.

Michael tore his lips from hers and kissed his way down her throat, murmuring, "Come home with me. Now."

His hands were on her breasts, caressing her through her shirt, his thumbs stroking her nipples to hardness. Isabelle ached to feel his hands on her skin; heat began to throb between her legs. *It had been so long.* All the passion, suppressed so many years, rose in her now; she was flooded with sensations, dazed by the desire pouring through her. Isabelle could do no more than whisper his name, her fingers moving frantically across his shoulders and tangling in his hair.

Michael could feel her trembling beneath his hands. He straightened and gazed down into her flushed, bemused face. The sight of her obvious arousal stirred him almost past bearing. "I'd like to sweep you up and carry you off," he told her huskily, "the way we always do in the show."

Isabelle opened her eyes and looked hazily at him, her eyes lambent with passion. "Then why don't you?"

Nine

Michael's breath came out in a shudder, and he bent and picked Isabelle up. Cradling her in his arms, he strode down the hall and around the corner. Isabelle wondered vaguely where he was taking her, but she didn't ask, only looped her arms around his neck and snuggled into him, planting soft feathery kisses on the side of his neck and face. Michael let out a soft groan, but he did not stop. He passed two soundstages and finally came to a halt before a door at the end of the corridor. Reaching down, he opened the door with a flick of his wrist and stepped inside, turning on a light switch as he did so.

A row of lights to the rear of the room came on, revealing a cavernous area filled with boxes and shelves containing all sorts of things, as well as pieces of furniture stacked and shoved into every part of the room. To one side was a large white cast-iron bed, draped with a gauzy material.

Michael set Isabelle down and reached behind him to lock the door. Isabelle looked over at the bed. She recognized it as the one in the stage set of Jessica's apartment when Isabelle first came on the show. She strolled over to the bed, smiling faintly.

"How did you know about this? I've never even been in the prop room before."

Michael followed her, wrapping his arms around her from behind and pulling her close. "Ah, that's the advantage of being friends with the crew."

He nuzzled her neck, then swept her up into his arms again and laid her on the bed. It was hard beneath her, for there was no mattress, only a covered mattress-size box, but Isabelle hardly even noticed. She was far too intent on Michael, who lay down beside her and kissed her. He took his time, letting his hands explore her body as his mouth possessed hers. Isabelle's hands roamed Michael's back and shoulders, caressing the smooth musculature beneath the cloth. She reveled in the feel of him, breathing in his scent.

But soon, as he kissed her, it was no longer enough to touch him through the shirt. Isabelle had to feel his flesh with her fingers. She pulled his shirt up, sliding her hands beneath it. Michael shivered and let out a soft noise of pleasure at her touch. Her fingers slid over his back, relearning each knob of bone, each dent and curve. She had thought she remembered the exact feel of his skin, but she realized now how much she had forgotten. His smooth flesh was more exciting than anything she could recall. Her fingers trembled, and she dug them into him, delighting when he drew his breath in with a hiss.

"Isabelle..." he murmured, burying his lips in her neck and moving slowly downward. "I have to see you... touch you."

He pulled her T-shirt up and off over her head, tossing it down on the bed. Her bra quickly followed it. He lay for a long moment, staring down at her bared breasts.

"You are so beautiful," he said thickly, and his forefinger traced the pinkish brown aureole of her nipple, watching the center tighten.

He curved his hand beneath her breast, holding it gently. He bent and kissed the pillowy soft top of the globe, then the crown, smiling as he felt it harden beneath his lips. His tongue came out and traced her nipple, coaxing the center bud to grow harder and longer.

Her tender flesh was alive to his every touch. As his mouth teased and caressed her, a fiery ache grew between her legs. Isabelle squeezed her legs together, seeking to satisfy the yearning, but could not. Only Michael could do that.

He took the hard button of her nipple into his mouth, sucking it, and Isabelle's whole body tightened in response. Michael moved his hand down her flat stomach, slipping beneath the loose waistband of her denim shorts and delving down into the hot, moist center of her desire. Isabelle instinctively pressed her pelvis up against his hand, moving rhythmically.

Hastily, with shaking fingers, Michael removed her shorts and panties. Isabelle, her breath coming hard and fast in her throat, tugged off Michael's shirt as he worked on her clothes, and she began to cover his chest with tiny hot kisses that made him moan. He slipped his hand between her legs, exploring the hot, slippery flesh. Isabelle dug her fingers into the bedspread beneath her as she raised her hips, urging him on. Desire was thrumming through her, building to an ever-higher peak, and when his clever fingers found the soft nub of flesh nestled secretly between the folds, she let out a choked cry. Softly he caressed the fleshy knot.

Isabelle moaned and whimpered, her head rolling back and forth on the pillow. She was almost mindless with hunger now. With each stroke of his fingers, he pushed her higher and higher. Then suddenly the passion burst inside her, surprising them both. Isabelle shuddered, letting out a choked cry, and her body went taut as the hunger exploded inside her, sending wave after wave of pleasure coursing through her body.

She went limp, dazed by the cataclysm. She looked up at Michael, her face soft and sated. He was looking down at her, his face taut and dark, his eyes fiery.

"Oh!" Isabelle blushed to her hairline as she realized what she had done. They had not even made love. All he had had to do was touch her, and she had leapt to her climax. "I'm sorry. You haven't—I mean—oh, God, you must think I'm—"

Michael smiled a trifle wolfishly. "I didn't mind. I enjoyed watching you."

"Oh, don't," Isabelle groaned, throwing her arm across her eyes to block him out. "I'm not usually so...so *needy*. You must think I'm awful."

"Not at all." He bent and brushed his lips across her bare stomach. "I think you're beautiful and excessively desirable, and I don't mind at all knowing that you've been just as much on the knife edge as I have been."

He stood up and skimmed out of the rest of his clothes, revealing his taut, hard body, his engorged manhood pulsing and stretching toward her.

"I have to be inside you," he said in a low voice, moving between her legs.

Her legs parted to accept him eagerly. His manhood nudged at the gate of her femininity, then moved slowly into her, stretching and filling her until she sobbed aloud with passion, her fingers digging into his back. The peace she had attained earlier was gone now, and she was filled once again with a roiling, aching hunger, a searing need that demanded to be satisfied.

Michael thrust rhythmically, pulling almost out, then plunging deep again. He moved slowly at first, drawing out every bit of pleasure from the friction, but as the tension grew in both of them, his hips pumped faster and faster, stoking their passion almost to the breaking point. Isabelle moaned, circling her pelvis against him, and her fingers dug into his back, heedless with desire. Michael let out a cry and stiffened as he reached his peak. He took her mouth in a deep kiss as his seed poured into her. Isabelle wrapped her legs tightly around him and clung to him, her own passion exploding through her in waves.

For one long moment they were lost in their cataclysmic pleasure, melded and mindless, pressed so tightly together that they seemed almost to be a part of each other. Then, slowly, they came back down into reality, their taut muscles relaxing.

Limp with satisfaction, Isabelle simply lay there, drifting in the afterglow of pleasure. It had been so long, so unbelievably long since she had felt like this. She wanted to cry and laugh and babble all at the same time, but she was too enervated to do any of those. A small smile curved her lips as she snuggled closer to Michael. He rolled onto his back, his arms still around her, holding her close, and they fell asleep.

Isabelle opened her eyes, and reality returned in a rush. *What time was it?* She had no watch, so she reached over and picked up Michael's wrist to look at his. It was almost seven-thirty! *She had forgotten about Jenny! Irma would have expected her back at least an hour ago, and if she was going to be working late, she always called to let her know.*

She was flooded with guilt. Isabelle scrambled out of bed and began to pick up her clothes. She pulled them on hurriedly, blushing as she glanced around the room. She thought about the fact that anyone in the prop department might have returned and entered the room with a key. *How had she let herself get so carried away?*

Isabelle knew that she had forgotten about her daughter in more ways than just getting home late tonight. Jenny was the thing that should be uppermost in her mind, but Isabelle had let her lust blind her to that fact. She had dropped all the hard-won decisions she had made in Mexico and simply fallen into Michael's arms. She had ignored Jenny and the future and all the problems, so now she was in an even worse mess.

She cast a troubled, yearning look back at Michael. *It had been so wonderful, being in his arms again, joined again in passion.* Isabelle wanted to cry. She knew she had to be responsible, mature; she had to do what was best for her and her child. But at the moment, what she longed to do was crawl back in bed with Michael and kiss him awake. She could imagine his mouth curving up into a languid smile, his eyes crinkling up in that certain way.

Almost as if her thoughts had been spoken out loud, Michael's eyes opened, and he glanced around, looking for her. He smiled sleepily when he saw her, just as she had pictured, and Isabelle's heart ached within her.

He linked his arms behind his head and asked, "What are you doing up?"

"I have to leave."

"You got an appointment?"

"Well, yes, actually, I was supposed to be home an hour ago." He quirked an eyebrow, and she added, "My daughter's baby-sitter will be worried. She'll want to leave."

"Your daughter? I didn't know you had any kids." The beginnings of a frown formed between his eyes.

Isabelle shrugged. "Well, it's—not anything we ever talked about. We haven't really talked much, you know."

"I know." He sat up, his face serious. "You're not married now, though, are you?"

"No. Look, this isn't pertinent, and I don't have time. I need to get home."

"Wait. Let me get dressed, and I'll come with you. I'll follow you home and I can meet your daughter, and then we can all go out to eat. How does that sound?"

"No!" Isabelle shook her head vigorously. "I'm sorry. It's just—well, I'm not sure this is a good idea. I don't want to take it too fast."

"Too fast?" His eyebrows lifted quizzically. "After ten years, you think we're going too fast?"

"I'm not talking about the past ten years. I'm talking about the past couple of weeks. Today. I—I'm not sure we did the right thing. I need to think about it."

He stared at her, stunned. "What's to think about? Isabelle... I think I'm falling in love with you all over again. Or maybe it's always been there, dormant. Sometimes I wonder if that wasn't the real reason I took this job—because I knew I'd see you again."

Isabelle shook her head again, sidling toward the door. "No. Michael, please..." She held out her hand, palm up. "Stop. I need to think about this. I didn't think this afternoon."

"No, you acted on instinct," he retorted. "You did what you really wanted to."

"I have to be sure! I have to consider more than just the temporary pleasure of making love with you! There's my daughter, and...and this job and...I'm not sure I'm ready to risk getting hurt again."

"This isn't the same as ten years ago!" Michael snapped in exasperation. "I'm not going to leave you!"

"Can you guarantee that?" Isabelle retorted. "I don't know if this is love or lust or just ending something that's been open for ten years. How can you be certain that you won't leave me when you aren't even sure whether or not you love me? You don't even know me anymore!"

"I would like to!" Michael swung out of bed and began pulling on his clothes with short, angry movements. "You won't let me. Anytime we get close, anytime you soften toward me and it looks like we might have a chance, you pull away again!"

Isabelle marched toward the door. In a way he was right; she didn't want him to know her because that meant knowing about Jenny, too.

"Dammit!" Michael exclaimed and went after her, clamping a hand around her arm and spinning Isabelle around to face him. He had had no time to put on anything more than his jeans, and even they were unbuttoned at the top.

Isabelle felt her eyes moving involuntarily down the smooth brown expanse of his chest, following the line of dark hair that curled down his chest to the well of his navel. She jerked her gaze away. But she found that she could not look into his blazing eyes, either.

"I'm not letting you run away!"

Isabelle straightened her spine, raising her chin, and stared resolutely back into his bright blue eyes. "I am not running away. I told you, I have to get home."

"Then let me come with you."

"No. Not tonight."

"When? Ever? Or are you going to pretend none of this happened, like you did in Mexico?"

"I didn't pretend none of it happened. I just didn't want it to go any further. And I was right—it didn't resolve anything. The same problems are still here."

"What problems? Your daughter? Our past? What is there that we can't talk about? That we can't work on?"

"I—I have to think," Isabelle repeated, disliking the little tremor she heard in her voice. "Give me a little time, Michael. I have to decide what's best for my daughter and me. I can't rush into things."

"Do I not have any say in the matter?"

"Yes, but—"

"But what?"

"I have to make the decision for me and for Jenny."

"Jenny? Is that your daughter?"

Isabelle nodded, wishing she hadn't given even that much away. She felt strangely vulnerable and scared. "Look, I'll call you. Give me some time to think it through, all right?" She tugged her arm out of his grasp. "I have to go now."

Quickly she unlocked the door and stepped through it into the hall. She almost ran down the corridor and out of the building.

Isabelle met Nancy the next day for lunch at a small exclusive café where they often ate. Isabelle had not seen her friend since before she went on location, so as soon as they had ordered, Isabelle began to relate everything that had happened in Cancún and since, ending with the final scene between her and Michael the night before. Nancy listened quietly, watching her, until at last Isabelle sat back and looked at her friend expectantly.

Nancy shoved her thick mass of red-gold curls back
from her face and sighed. "Maybe I'm stupid, but I don'
understand. Why shouldn't you and Michael have a re
lationship? I mean, you two obviously still have feeling;
for each other."

"Lust, Nance. That's not the same thing as liking o
respect or anything that you can build a real relationshi;
on."

"I know quite a few relationships that started out tha
way—and they didn't all go down the tubes, either, sc
don't give me that look. Maybe it won't go anywhere
maybe it's just unfinished business left over from te;
years ago, but even if it is, wouldn't you feel better if yo
went ahead and found out? At least you'd be able to clos
it for good, then. As it is, you're going to always won
der."

"Why are you so eager for me to have an affair witl
Michael Traynor?" Isabelle asked in exasperation
"You'd think you were his cheerleading squad."

"No, I'm yours," her friend replied simply.

"Then why would you want to see me get back to
gether with somebody who dumped me before?"

"You told me that you had forgiven him, that you un
derstood why he did it. I don't see why you can't let it go
too. After all, Michael was young and foolish. Twenty-
three is not exactly a mature adult. And if he was trying
to do the right thing, to act responsibly—"

"So he wasn't a feelingless ogre. That doesn't mean I
have to jump back in bed with him."

"You already did that," Nancy commented wryly.

"You know what I mean. I don't have to let it go any
further than last night."

"True. But you don't have to cut it off, either. Why no
see what develops?" When Isabelle continued to look a

her skeptically, Nancy leaned forward and said, "Look, this is the first guy I've ever seen stir you up this way. Since the day he walked onto that soundstage, you have been talking and thinking about nothing but him. I've known you for years, and I've never seen you this bothered about any man. What I'm thinking is that maybe this guy is what you really need."

"I need to be bothered and upset all the time?" Isabelle retorted.

"A little wouldn't hurt. At least it would prove that you're alive."

Isabelle frowned at her friend. "What's that supposed to mean?"

"Only that you need something in your life besides your job and Jenny."

"I'm happy with my life. Or at least I was until Michael showed up here."

"And reminded you of what you're missing. Isabelle, everyone needs love—not just maternal love or the love between friends, either. You need romantic love, as well. This is the first time that you've acted like you might have found it. Didn't you enjoy last night?"

Isabelle was unaware of the way her face softened. "It was wonderful."

"Then do something for yourself for once. See what develops."

"And what if it develops that Michael decides that it's 'for the best' for him to move on again?"

"Ah, so you haven't completely forgiven him, have you?"

"Maybe not. I don't know. I think—I think that I've forgiven him, but I can't forget it. It happened, and even if his motives were good, that doesn't mean that it won't happen again. I was devastated when he left me last time. Destroyed. I won't allow that to happen again."

"You don't have to commit yourself for life to the guy. Try going out on a date, something ordinary like that. See where it leads. You may find that you don't even like him anymore, that it's just the bittersweet memory that appeals to you."

Isabelle shook her head. "It's too scary." She sighed and ran a hand back through her hair. "I'm afraid that if I let him into my life even one little inch, it'll be like before. You don't know the effect he has on me. If you had ever kissed this guy, you'd know what I was talking about."

"But that's the way it's supposed to be. That's what everybody's looking for, isn't it?"

"Oh, yeah, it's great until you crash and burn. And it's not only me who will get hurt this time. There's Jenny to consider. You know how hard I try to keep her life safe and sane, to protect her from publicity, keep everything orderly and smooth."

"I know. You've done a wonderful job."

"Well, what's it going to do to her if Michael comes sweeping into our life?"

"There's nothing wrong with her learning to share her mother. And don't you think it might be a good thing for her to get to know her father, too?"

"No!" Isabelle's eyes flashed. "I'm not hauling Michael in and saying, 'Sweetheart, here's your daddy.' I just told you, I don't want her disturbed."

"Change doesn't mean the same thing as disturb, necessarily. It could be a good experience for Jenny. Besides, doesn't he have a right to know that he has a child?"

"He hasn't known up till now, and he's done okay," Isabelle replied defensively. "I am her parent, the only one she's ever known. I've raised her, done everything for her. And she's done just fine."

"Of course she has. I'm not saying that you haven't done a great job. But you won't be any less her mother if she has a father, too."

"He doesn't need to know. He doesn't have the right. He went off and left me—" Isabelle stopped and sighed. Nancy had touched her on a sore spot. She had felt guilty more than once when she looked at Michael and thought about the fact that he had a daughter he knew nothing about.

"All right," Isabelle admitted, "I know I'm being unfair. Michael didn't know I was pregnant. He's never known about Jenny, so I can't blame him for ignoring her. Maybe it would be fairer if I told him about Jenny, but that's not my first priority. Jenny's welfare is. What if he sees her and doesn't want her? What if he rejects her?"

Isabelle quailed inside at the thought; it seemed as if something inside of her would shrivel up and die if Michael rejected Jenny.

"I know you've have one or two bad experiences with men who were put off by Jenny," Nancy said. "But you don't know how Michael's going to react. Don't tell her he's her father until after you know how he feels about it. Maybe you could let him meet Jenny and not even tell him until you see how he reacts to her. He just might love her, too, you know. After all, she's a pretty lovable little kid. Michael might be a wonderful addition to her life."

"What if he does want to be her father? What if she comes to love him and depend on him? Then what's going to happen to her, how's she going to feel, if he de-

cides to leave? What if he gets a great part in New Yor
or in a movie, shooting on location? He'd be gone like
shot. An actor's career always comes first. Whateve
wonderful reasons he had for not taking me with hi
when he left Virginia, one thing he did *not* consider wa
not going. The part was more important—I've never me
an actor to whom it wasn't.''

"Maybe that's true. And maybe it's not. I don't kno
the guy that well. But I do know one thing. Jenny is no
as fragile as you think. You don't have to wrap her up i
cotton her whole life."

"I'm not trying to do that. You know I don't smothe
Jenny. She goes to school. She goes to that camp for tw
weeks in the summer."

"I know that. You're a wonderful mother—I'm no
questioning that. You want Jenny's life to be as perfec
as you can possibly make it. But people can't be happy a
the time. Jenny can't be any more than you or I car
She's going to have hardships and sorrows and disap
pointments. It's part of being a human being. If you tr
to protect her from all those things, then you're not let
ting her be a real person."

"You think I should knowingly let her get hurt—whe
I can keep her from it?"

"I think sometimes you have to let her have her ow
life experiences and not shield her from everything. Le
her live a little life without knowing whether it's going t
be happy or sad, just like everyone else does." She pause
and looked meaningfully at Isabelle. "And maybe yo
have to let yourself do that, too. You and Jenny can't liv
in a glass bubble."

Isabelle gazed at her friend for a long moment. *Coul.
Nancy be right? Was she wrong to keep Jenny from he
father? Was she smothering Jenny by protecting her s*

much? And was she herself rejecting love and joy just because there might be pain involved in it?

Isabelle drove home from their lunch slowly, thinking about everything that Nancy had said. She didn't want to believe it; she had never thought of herself as cowardly. But something inside told her that Nancy had been right, that it was fear that kept her from Michael, fear that made her try to keep herself and Jenny locked in a private world.

She got out of her car and walked inside the house. Irma, sitting in the kitchen, reading a magazine, smiled and got up to leave. Isabelle said goodbye to her and walked on through the house to the family room, where Jenny sat playing with a friend from school. Jenny saw her and jumped up to come give her a hug. Her friend Carla followed suit. Isabelle hugged them both, and the two girls returned to their dolls.

Isabelle stood watching them, idly reaching down to scratch Prudence when she came up to wind around Isabelle's ankles in greeting. Jenny was such a loving child; Isabelle could not remember anyone that Jenny didn't immediately accept. Jenny would love Michael if he didn't turn away from her. She had none of the fear that kept Isabelle frozen into her patterns.

Isabelle turned away and went into her bedroom. She called Carol Nieman and then dialed the number Carol had given her. After two rings, Michael's voice answered.

"Michael?" Isabelle asked quickly. She hoped he didn't recognize the nervousness in her voice. "This is Isabelle."

"Yes, I know." There was a wariness in his tone.

Fear touched Isabelle's heart. *Had he decided not to put up with her uncertainties? Had he cut himself off from her?*

"I—I wanted to ask you—that is, I'm fixing, uh, lasagna tonight for Jenny and me, and I thought, well, would you like to come?"

Isabelle thought she heard the slightest sound on the other end, like a quickly indrawn or released breath. Then Michael replied quietly, "Yes. I'd like to very much."

Ten

The doorbell rang, and Isabelle started toward the front door, wiping her damp palms down the sides of her skirt. She was as nervous as a girl on her first date, she thought.

Would Michael be put off by Jenny, as some of the other men she'd dated had been? It would be painful to lose him, to have the new delicate shoots of caring chopped away and the soaring passion that they shared, ended. Worse than that, though, would be the disillusionment. It would hurt to discover that he didn't have the strength or compassion to accept Jenny.

And would he recognize Jenny as his daughter? Isabelle wasn't sure. Because she was quite small for her age, and looked younger, judging from her size, he might think it was impossible that she was his. Jenny could have gotten her coloring from Isabelle herself as easily as from her father; Isabelle's hair was as dark as either Jenny's or Michael's, and Jenny's skin was pale, like Isabelle's. It was harder, Isabelle knew, to see one's own resemblance to someone else. But those eyes! Could anyone look at Jenny and not see that her intense blue eyes with the startlingly thick, straight black eyebrows above them were exactly like Michael's own?

She could only hope that he would not, for then either course could be painful. He might want to have nothing to do with Jenny, have no feelings for her, and that would be like a knife to Isabelle's heart. Or he might want to be with Jenny, to acknowledge her as his daughter, but then if he left, Jenny would be devastated.

Isabelle opened the door. Michael was standing there, and for a moment they faced each other a little uncertainly. The way they had parted the other night left them both tentative.

"Isabelle." Michael stepped inside, hesitated, then bent to kiss her.

Isabelle answered by tilting up her face to his kiss. A shaky little sigh escaped him, and Michael's kiss was deep and searching. He pulled Isabelle to him, pressing her into his body. When at last he released her and Isabelle stepped back, they were both a trifle flushed and breathing unevenly.

Patience, who had followed Isabelle to the door, interrupted them by squirming in between their legs and rearing back on her hind legs to greet Michael. She planted her forepaws on his leg and seemed to grin up at him, her tail wagging furiously. Michael glanced down at his new admirer and smiled.

"Hey, there." He reached down and stroked Patience's head, scratching that certain spot behind her ears that sent her into a state of pure bliss. "Quite a watchdog you've got here," he remarked.

"Only if a burglar could be licked to death."

Jenny came into the entry. She stopped and gazed at Michael in that solemn, unnerving way she had. "Hi."

Michael smiled at her. "Hi. I'm Michael Traynor. You must be Isabelle's daughter."

He held out his hand to her to shake, and Jenny took it gingerly. "I'm Jenny."

"It's nice to meet you, Jenny."

"You want to see my bike?" she asked. "I can take Patience for a ride on it."

"Can you?" Michael looked interested and impressed. "How do you get her to stay on?"

"She sits in her basket. Sometimes she jumps out."

"I see."

Jenny was already leading Michael down the hall and through the kitchen, to the door leading into the garage, where her three-wheeler was parked. Isabelle followed them, her stomach twitching nervously.

"Here it is." Jenny pointed to her bicycle.

"Mmm-hmm." Michael inspected it from all sides. "It's big, isn't it? You must be strong to handle it."

Jenny nodded her head emphatically. "That's the truth," she said, her voice an uncanny imitation of Isabelle. "I had trouble at first. But you just have to get back on. When you fall off, you just have to get back on."

"That's right."

"You want to see me ride it?"

"Sure. You going to take the dog?"

"Patience," Jenny corrected him. "Her name is Patience. We used to have Lady, but they took her. Lady's in Heaven now. She was sick, and Mom took her." Jenny made a gesture with her hands as though drawing a rectangle. "To that place. And the doctor said she was too sick. So they took her there. Lady's in Heaven now."

Michael nodded. "She's probably happier there."

"Yes." Jenny nodded. "She was sick. Mom cried. But she's better in Heaven. And we have Patience now."

This was a subject that Jenny could ramble on about forever, so Isabelle said, "Why don't you show Michael how you can ride your bike, Jenny?"

"Okay." She started wheeling her bike out of the garage, saying, "I can ride it real good."

"I'm sure you can," Michael responded.

Jenny picked up the uncomplaining Patience and stowed her in the basket on the back of the vehicle. Then she climbed on carefully and started pedaling up and down the driveway. Michael watched her, smiling, and when she came near them again, he said, "You're good on that bike."

"I know." Jenny started down the drive again.

Michael turned toward Isabelle. "Your daughter is delightful."

Isabelle felt foolishly like crying. "You—you were very good with her."

"I like her," he said simply.

"I'm glad." Her smile was a little tremulous.

Michael slipped his arm around Isabelle's shoulders and pulled her close against his side. "I take it you've been with other guys who didn't like her?"

"I wasn't with them long," Isabelle replied dryly.

Michael let out a bark of laughter. "So this was sort of a litmus test for me?"

"I don't know if it's a test, exactly, but...well, it's pretty impossible to go anywhere with a man who's repulsed by my child."

"Repulsed? Surely you don't mean that. How could someone be repulsed by Jenny? She's a sweet girl."

He obviously meant what he said; he was genuinely amazed that someone might not want to be around Jenny. He wasn't just being polite or acting. He liked her daughter just as she was.

Isabelle relaxed, letting out a small sigh of relief. "There are people who are repulsed. Or scared of her. Not everyone is able to handle being around people who are handicapped, either mentally or physically. I don't know what it is exactly, but you can see the uneasiness in their eyes, in the way they stand. It's as though they know they shouldn't show it, but they have to brace themselves not to. They don't realize it at first—she looks fine, you know. But then you can see the understanding dawning on them as they talk to her, and there is this subtle body language, a sort of drawing up. Other people are simply too impatient to deal with her. They can't stand the repetition and the chatter."

Michael shook his head. "It doesn't bother me. I like kids. I always wanted a family. I guess it's from all those years I spent bumping around from foster home to foster home. Never belonging anywhere."

There was a distant look in his eyes for a moment, and Isabelle felt a sympathetic tightening in her chest. "I remember your telling me how much you hated it."

"I always swore I'd be the best dad ever. Even when I was a teenager, I'd think about how I'd do things with my kids...teach them stuff." He shrugged. "Now here I am—never had any."

Guilt wriggled through Isabelle. *Had she been wrong to withhold Jenny from him all these years?* Isabelle sidestepped the subject. "You were married, though. I saw an article about it."

Michael cast her a humorous glance. "Checking up on me, eh?"

Isabelle flushed faintly. "Well, sometimes I'd see something about you, and I'd read it. I was curious, I'll admit it."

"So was I. I read everything about you I ever saw." He looked at her for a long moment, then turned away, looking out across the yard toward Jenny. "It's true. I was married for about a year. It was one of those dumb, totally mismatched things. We got married four or five years ago, and then we discovered we didn't get along. I wanted kids—that was one of the reasons I wanted to marry. It was really important to me to have a big family. But Annie didn't want any. She didn't bother to tell me that she didn't intend to have a family until after we were married. But as soon as I suggested that she go off the Pill, she let me know in no uncertain terms that she had no intention of letting pregnancy spoil her figure. But she was just as unwilling to adopt or have foster children or anything of that nature. Kids would cramp her style. She wanted to party all night and sleep half the day and spend the rest of her time shopping. I don't know how we were ever attracted to each other in the first place. I was glad to call it quits." He shrugged. "She was glad to get alimony."

"I'm sorry."

"It didn't hurt like it did when I left you," he said simply. He paused, then went on. "What about you? Are you divorced from Jenny's father?"

Isabelle shook her head. "No. We were never married."

The subject made her nervous; she wasn't ready yet to tell Michael that he was Jenny's father—especially not after he'd told her how much he had wanted children. She had the uneasy feeling that he would be furious with her for concealing Jenny's existence. Whatever was developing between them seemed too tender and fragile to withstand more anger from the past. Besides, she wasn't yet sure enough of Michael to expose Jenny to the hurt that could result.

She shifted uneasily and said, "I'd rather not talk about him."

"All right." Michael paused, watching Jenny driving around in endless circles at the far end of the driveway. "Tell me about Jenny."

"Well, she goes to a special school, and she's doing wonderfully well. She almost never throws temper tantrums anymore. She used to get very angry, you see, when she was frustrated or when you'd cross her about something, and she would shout and kick and hit, even bite. But she's gotten better as she's gotten older, and since she's been at this school, she's almost completely overcome it. She has learned not to pick up everything and put it in her mouth, and she can stop talking for several minutes or go play by herself for a while if you tell her firmly to do it. She's pretty high-level. They tell me when she's older she should be able to live in a halfway house and be semi-independent. Hold down a job."

"You look sad when you say that."

Isabelle made a wry face. "I'll miss her. I guess it will be best for her, to be around other people, to live more like a regular adult. But I know I'll be lonely for her."

Michael ran a caressing hand down her hair. She turned and looked up at him to find that he was gazing at her, his face warm and tender. "You're a very loving mother. There are some who would have given up long ago on the trouble and effort of raising her, who would have sent her away to some private institution."

Isabelle smiled wryly. "I'm not a saint. There have been many times when I was frustrated and tired and impatient with her. Besides, it's much easier when you can afford to have good help to care for her whenever you're not home, or to send her to expensive day schools."

"There were plenty of years before you were starring in a soap," he pointed out. "It had to be tough then. And it's only human to get frustrated or impatient. The thing is, you loved her enough to overcome those things."

"She's my daughter. How could I not?"

Michael bent and placed a gentle kiss on Isabelle's lips. "That's what's so special, that you don't think it is, that you wouldn't have thought of anything else."

"Wouldn't you have done the same thing?"

"You mean, if Jenny were my daughter?" He paused, considering. Isabelle liked him for that, that he didn't just automatically, carelessly, agree. "Yes," he said after a moment. "I would have done the same thing."

Guilt gnawed at Isabelle. *She ought to tell him.* But again she backed away. It wasn't time yet. There was no telling what might happen between her and Michael. She would wait until she was sure.

Jenny came pedaling back up to them. "I'm hungry," she announced, coming to a halt.

"I imagine supper's about ready," Isabelle replied, happy to change the subject. "Why don't we go inside and see?"

Jenny climbed off her bike and took Patience out of the basket. Patience shook herself off and gratefully bounded away, then back, and jumped up to greet Michael all over again.

Jenny took Michael's hand as they started into the house, saying proudly, "I helped with supper."

"Did you? Then I imagine it will really be good, won't it?"

Jenny nodded her head emphatically. "I like lasagna. It's my favorite." She paused, considering. "Almost. I like pizza better."

Michael grinned. "Me, too. I'm a pizza junkie."

Jenny began a long, disjointed recital about one time when the pizza man came. Even Isabelle wasn't sure what she was talking about. But Michael listened patiently, and when the story became hopelessly tangled, he managed to direct Jenny onto another subject.

Isabelle took the lasagna out of the oven and carried it to the table, while Jenny proudly showed Michael the place settings she had arranged. He complimented her and, Isabelle was pleased to note, did not reorganize the haphazard arrangement of silverware into the more customary setting, as more than one guest had done in the past.

They sat down to eat in the breakfast room off the kitchen. Isabelle cast a glance around the small room and commented, "We're a little informal here."

She didn't add that they rarely used the formal dining room because of Jenny's frequent spills. Tile was much easier to clean up.

Michael smiled and poured her a glass of wine. "That's the way I like it."

Isabelle chuckled. "You're very agreeable tonight."

He cast her a wounded look. "Are you implying that I'm not always that way?" He shrugged. "Anyway, it's easy to be agreeable here. Everything—and everyone—is just right."

There was a warmth in his eyes as he looked at Isabelle that made color tinge her cheeks. Even in this prosaic setting, with Jenny sitting beside them, Michael could stir her passion with no more than a glance.

The meal was blissfully ordinary. They talked and laughed as they ate, and Jenny was happy to join in their laughter even though she understood little of the humor. Isabelle had never cared much for the trappings of being an actress. She didn't want to dine at Spago or put on a designer dress and jewels and go out to be seen. She was far more content in jeans and a T-shirt, having a meal at home with Jenny, and Michael seemed to be as comfortable with it as she.

Please let it be true, she found herself thinking now and then throughout the meal. There had been other men who had pretended an interest in Jenny, who had seemed to be pleased to act "like ordinary people," but who had really been interested only in getting into bed with Isabelle. The passion was there with Michael; there was no doubt about that. She could see it each time he looked at her, feel it whenever he touched her arm or her hand. But along with the banked desire, there was also a certain easiness, a sense of being natural and right.

After supper, they sat in the family room, feet up on the coffee table, hands clasped, and they talked while Jenny watched TV. They talked about the years since they had parted and the things that had happened to them. Michael listened, his thumb rubbing Isabelle's hand soothingly, as she told him about Jenny's birth and the long months of hope and fear afterward. Tears sparkled in her eyes, and he wrapped an arm around her shoulders, pulling her close to him. Isabelle leaned against his chest, breathing in his scent, luxuriating in the comfort of his arms around her. She was falling in love with him, she thought, and she hoped it wasn't foolish. But she sensed that, whether is was wise or not, she couldn't stop herself.

Later in the evening, Isabelle put Jenny to bed, despite Jenny's reluctance. Jenny insisted on giving Michael a hug and a kiss before she went. When Isabelle returned, Michael stretched up a hand and took Isabelle's wrist, pulling her down onto his lap. She snuggled up against him, her head on his shoulder, his arm around her back. He nuzzled her hair, and a shiver ran down Isabelle's spine. She was very aware of his hard chest and the heat of his body. Isabelle smoothed a hand across his shoulder and down his arm.

She thought about her bedroom, which lay on the other side of the house from Jenny's. She had always thought that she would never let a man spend the night here. It had been an easy decision, she realized now, because she had never before found a man who tempted her to anything else. But now she found herself thinking that Jenny would never know, as long as Michael left before she got up the next morning.

Still, she stirred uneasily and sat up, leaning away from Michael and shaking her head. "Michael, I . . ."

"I know." He cupped her chin and kissed her, firmly but without passion. "I understand. You feel uneasy with your daughter so close. I'm not pushing you. Let's just sit here and talk for a while."

So they did, talking some of the time and the rest of the time just sitting in warm, silent, closeness. Desire hummed deliciously beneath the surface, and now and then they kissed or caressed, but they did not allow their passion to break through and carry them away. There was something sweetly exciting about postponing their lovemaking, a certain fulfillment in simply being with one another.

Later Isabelle made them coffee and they talked some more, this time sitting mundanely in the kitchen. Finally, reluctantly, they parted, barely able to keep their eyes open, yet hating to let the other one go. Isabelle could remember many nights like that ten years ago, when they had said long goodbyes on the front porch of her boardinghouse, reluctant to part even after being together for hours.

"I feel like a teenager again," Isabelle murmured as she walked with Michael to the front door, their hands linked together.

He smiled and raised her hand to his lips. "You look like one, too."

They stopped at the door, and he turned, leaning back against it, and pulled Isabelle into his arms. He kissed her face, methodically moving from forehead to cheeks to nose to chin and finally settling lovingly on her mouth. They kissed until she was breathless; then Michael tore his mouth away and rested his head against hers.

"I could almost believe that being with you is enough," he murmured, "but it's not." He kissed her ear, his teeth and lips teasing at the fleshy lobe. "I want you so much."

His breath tickled her ear, stirring her even more, and Isabelle moved her body restlessly against his. "I want you, too."

"Can I see you tomorrow night?" He grinned. "We can practice our scene for Monday."

He referred to the big love scene they would film on Monday, in which Jessica and Curtis finally made love in a supposed cave in the jungle. Heat twisted in Isabelle's abdomen at just the thought of it.

"All right," she whispered, laying a soft kiss on his chin.

"At my place." He kissed the side of her neck.

Isabelle drew in her breath sharply. "Yes."

She pulled back, her eyes glittering in the dim light of the entry. "You better go now."

"I will." He pulled her to him for another deep, long kiss, then with a muffled curse, pulled away from her and went out the door.

Isabelle closed the door behind him and turned, leaning against the door as he had done. She closed her eyes, indulging herself in all the wonderful sensations that were coursing through her. Tomorrow couldn't get here soon enough, she thought and, smiling, she walked through the house to her bedroom, turning off the lights.

"I like Michael," Jenny announced the next morning, slathering peach jelly on her toast.

"Do you? I'm glad. So do I." Isabelle stood at the sink, scraping off her own breakfast plate.

"Are you going to marry him?"

Isabelle whirled and stared at her daughter. "Jenny! Whatever made you think such a thing?"

Jenny shrugged. "I don't know. Brandon's dad got married."

"Oh, he did?" Isabelle relaxed a little.

Jenny nodded in her emphatic way. "Yeah. And he got to... got to... sit. There, in front. He didn't snort."

"Well, good."

"He was not supposed to. His dad said, he said, 'No snorting.'" She turned her hands up in a quizzical gesture. "And he said he didn't. The lady wore, you know..." She stood and gestured in sweeping motions down her legs.

"A wedding dress?" Isabelle guessed.

"Yes. And her head was all..." She made circular motions. "You'd look pretty with it."

"Thank you, Jenny, but I don't have any plans to get married anytime soon."

"I like Michael," Jenny reiterated.

"I know. He likes you, too." Isabelle came over and sat down across the table from her daughter. "I have to go to Michael's this afternoon. Mrs. Pena will be here in a little while to take care of you."

"Can I come?"

"Not today. Michael and I are going to run lines for our scene tomorrow. So we have to be alone."

"Oh." Jenny paused, then went on, apparently captivated by her previous topic. "You'd be prettier than Brandon's new mom."

"Thank you, but let's not talk about a wedding or a bride for a while, okay? Let's talk about what you and I are going to do before Mrs. Pena comes. What would you like to do?"

"Plant flowers," Jenny replied promptly. "I couldn't help the man. Mrs. Pena said, 'No, don't talk.' I can dig good, though."

"I know you can. Let's do that, then."

They spent the rest of the morning digging in the garden, planting flowers, as Jenny had wanted. Afterward, Isabelle showered and dressed, more careful than she usually was about her makeup and clothes. She still dressed casually—her wardrobe consisted of little besides jeans, shorts and tops, since after her usual day spent in glamorous dresses, jewelry, hose and torturous high heels, she favored casual wear. But today she spent fifteen minutes trying on jeans and tops until she found exactly the combination that she wanted.

She drove to Michael's condo, feeling a little nervous. It was silly, she knew, but somehow she couldn't help but feel that last night had been merely a dream, her imagi-

ation, and that this afternoon they would once more be
at odds.

But Michael opened the door before she got to it, almost as soon as she parked and got out of her car, and
the smile on his face was enough to light up a room. Isabelle hurried the last few steps to him and, as he opened
his arms to her, she almost jumped into them. They came
together in a blazing kiss. Michael's arms went around
Isabelle, lifting her up against his chest until her feet
dangled off the ground and, never breaking their kiss, he
walked with her inside the apartment and shut the door.

Eleven

———

They undressed with frantic haste, making their wa
blindly through the apartment, unable to cease thei
kisses long enough to finish taking off a garment or tak
more than a few steps. Their mouths clung, tongue
twining around one another in a dance of passion, an
their hands roamed over each other almost desperately
Isabelle backed into a chair, and Michael reached aroun
her to shove it out of the way.

Then they came up hard against a wall, but they didn'
seem to mind it. Michael pressed his body into Isa
belle's, his forearms braced upon the wall, and he tore hi
mouth from hers to trail kisses down her neck. Hi
breathing was hard and labored, as if he had been run
ning, and the sound of it sent a tremor of desire streak
ing down into Isabelle's abdomen.

"I couldn't sleep last night," Michael murmure
huskily. "I kept thinking about today, about this."

Isabelle felt as if her bones were melting. She clung to him, digging her fingers into the muscles of his back. "Michael," she whispered dazedly. "Please..."

"Oh, I will." He paused long enough to look into her face, a grin of sexual anticipation curving his mouth. "I guarantee I will please you."

"Will you?" She smiled hazily, her mouth soft and faintly swollen from their kisses. "I'd like that."

A groan escaped him, and he kissed her again, his hand coming up her front and sliding under the blouse he had already unbuttoned. His hand spread over her breast, caressing it through the delicate satin and lace of her bra. Pushing apart the sides of her shirt, he bent and took her breast in his mouth, suckling it through the flimsy material. When he raised his head, the damp cloth was molded to her nipple; it stood out dark and pointing. Michael gazed at it, desire flushing his face, then bent and brushed his lips across the swollen bud, making it tighten and prickle even more, thrusting eagerly toward his mouth.

He teased at her nipple until Isabelle was panting, her head twisting restlessly against the wall and her fingers clawing at his shoulders. Michael blew softly upon the damp center, and at Isabelle's quick, indrawn breath, he smiled. "Does that please you?"

Isabelle pushed against him with her pelvis in answer, circling her hips slowly, and Michael shuddered violently. There were no questions after that, no words except the brief, incoherent murmurings of passion. He ripped the blouse back and down her arms and fumbled frantically with the clasp of her brassiere. Finally he got it, and her breasts tumbled free. He cupped them in his hands and bent his head to kiss them, gently kneading the soft orbs as his mouth and tongue tasted every inch.

He pulled back, and they tore at the remaining piece
of their clothing, flinging them to the ground. They cam
back together, in too great a frenzy to seek the comfo:
of his bed, and sank down upon the floor, kissing an
caressing. Michael traced the line of her body with h
lips, moving with velvety kisses down from her shou
der, over her breast and onto the flat plain of her ston
ach, then to the sensitive soft skin of her abdomen. H
skimmed across the point of her hipbone, onto her thig
and downward to her foot. Isabelle twisted and stretche
in a pleasure so great, it was almost agony. Everywher
he touched, fever exploded in her; she wanted him to g
on forever, yet she wanted him to stop immediately an
give her the satisfaction she craved.

He made his way back up her leg, this time his lij
tracking up the inside of her calf and thigh. Isabell
quivered, whispering his name and twining her hand
urgently in his hair. As his tongue traced whorls upon he
inner thigh, his hand came up and touched the nest c
hair between her legs. Gently he separated the folds c
flesh, exploring them and finding the little nub that wa
the center of her pleasure. He moved his thumb over th
button softly, delighting in the slick wetness that wa
proof of her passion for him.

Isabelle stiffened and groaned as his hand stoked he
desire, bringing her nearer and nearer to her peak. The
his hand was gone and his mouth was upon her. She fe'
herself spinning away into a maelstrom of passion.

''Please,'' she murmured. ''I want you inside me.''

Her plea was too much for him to resist. Quickly M
chael positioned himself between her opened legs an
thrust into her, groaning at the exquisite pleasure of be
ing embedded deep within her soft, tight flesh. He be
gan to move with long, slow strokes, but desire lashe

him forward, and he thrust more quickly. Isabelle tightened her arms and legs around him, feeling the storm gather within her and then explode. She shuddered, clinging tightly to Michael, and the tiny movements of her body sent him hurtling forward into his own explosion. He groaned, burying himself within her, and bucked wildly. They clung together, lost in the wild, dark world of their united passion, transported for that moment into a place of joy so vibrant, so strong that memories of it were invariably only pale copies.

At last they relaxed with long sighs of fulfillment, and Michael rolled off her, pulling her into his arms and cradling her. They lay in stunned exhaustion.

"Well," Michael said lightly, "if we do this often enough today, perhaps I won't embarrass myself again tomorrow by turning hard as a rock in front of the camera."

Isabelle chuckled. "And maybe we'll be able to rehearse this afternoon without interruption."

But it was some time before they got to their rehearsal, for they arose after long, lazy minutes of idle talking and repleted kisses. Then they went into the bathroom to shower. Since they took the shower together, it was not long before their bodies were tingling with excitement again.

Michael washed Isabelle carefully, not missing an inch. Isabelle took her time rubbing lather all over his chest and stomach and down his long legs and back up. Then she picked up the soap and worked up the lather again and set to work on his buttocks and then his abdomen. Careful to reach every bit of him, her soapy hand even delved gently between his legs. Michael sucked in a breath and dug his hands into her hair, but Isabelle merely gave him a smile full of sexual teasing and proceeded to rinse off his body with equal thoroughness.

When his skin was squeaky clean, he turned off the water and started to get out, but Isabelle stopped him with a hand on his chest. "Wait, it's still my turn. You made love to me last time. Let me make love to you."

She began her exploration of his body with her mouth. Taking her time about it, she kissed her way over his chest to the small masculine nipples. Her mouth fastened on each of them in turn, her lips rubbing them into tight, hard buttons until Michael was gasping with delight. Then she circled each one with her tongue, lightly flicking them into even greater tautness, and finally settled her mouth firmly on one and began to suck.

Michael's fingers dug into her buttocks, lifting her almost off her feet in his paroxysm of pleasure. Isabelle lifted her face up to him, eyes innocently wide. "Do you want me to stop?"

"No," he groaned. "Please, no, don't stop."

She went back to minister to the other tight bud, and her hand slipped down his wet body. She curled her fingers around his engorged manhood, smiling as she felt it surge and pulse against her hand.

"Mmm, you're not wasting any time, are you?" she murmured.

"I can't do anything else with you," he replied, reaching out to push open the shower door.

"No. Not yet," she admonished. "I'm not finished."

He groaned again, but his hand dropped to his side and he waited, his skin taut and trembling with eagerness as she went back to her ministrations. Standing back a little and watching him, Isabelle moved her hands freely over his slick body, sliding down his chest and abdomen and around to his buttocks. She kneaded the muscled lesh and slid her fingers farther down onto his thighs. Her hands came back up and slipped between his legs, lightly cupping him.

Michael bit his lip with his teeth, letting out a muffled curse. She began to kiss her way down his abdomen, drawing ever closer to the thickened, throbbing seat of his passion.

He muttered something thickly and reached down, lifting her with his hands beneath her buttocks. He kissed her deeply, his tongue thrusting into her mouth as he parted her legs and thrust into her. Isabelle wrapped her legs around him and began to circle her hips, as frenzied as he to complete their passion. Pressing her against the tile wall of the shower, he moved inside her, thrusting with hard, desperate strokes, as if he sought to bury himself in the very center of her soul. They moved wildly, gasping and uttering unintelligible sounds, until at last they reached the wild burst of pleasure that they sought.

Hoarsely, Michael let out a cry, burying it against Isabelle's mouth as they erupted into a white-hot explosion.

They drifted down from the peak of pleasure, falling by slow degrees into their separate selves again. They stood, leaning against the shower wall, hazy and numbed.

Finally Michael let out a soft chuckle and rested his forehead against Isabelle's. "You know, I'm beginning to think that we're never going to make love in the comfort of a real bed."

"I don't know," Isabelle replied, sliding down to stand again and smiling impishly up at him. "Somehow I suspect that we'll get another chance to do that before I leave here today."

She was right, for they made love again after they rehearsed, as excited and stirred as if they had not already come together twice in passion that day. They made love in his bed this time, slowly and leisurely stoking the fires of their ardor until they melted into a warm union, as sweet and gentle as their previous ones had been frenzied and explosive.

Afterward, they lay together on the bed, lazily talking about Jenny, the cast of their show, the costumes, L.A., New York—whatever drifted into their minds. They ate cheese and fruit, sitting cross-legged on his bed, accompanying it with a delicate white wine. Isabelle wished that the afternoon would go on forever, that she did not have to leave. But she had to, she knew; Jenny was waiting for her.

Isabelle dressed, and Michael pulled on his clothes, too, so that he could walk her out to her car. She got in, and he bent down to kiss her through the open window. Tears caught in her throat. She thought that she would never experience anything again as sweet and wild and utterly wonderful as this afternoon. The words *I love you* rose unexpectedly to her lips, but she bit them back. *It was too soon, far too soon for that, no matter what her impulsive heart told her.*

She said only, "Goodbye," and drove away.

Isabelle couldn't remember a time when she had been so happy. She had been wrong to think that that particular afternoon at Michael's apartment could never be equaled. It was never exactly the same, of course, but there were many more times that were just as full of happiness or pleasure.

The show was a delight now that she no longer had to dread her scenes with Michael. It was fun to work with him, and the chemistry between them was electrifying. As soon as the jungle scenes began to air, the "Tomorrows" ratings soared. When the big love scene in the cave aired, the show shoved "Eden Crossing" out of the number-one spot in the ratings. Danny and Carol were ecstatic, and they were even more so when "All Our Tomorrows" remained in that position.

The fan mail poured in. Everyone either loved or hated the pairing of the wicked Jessica and the saintly Curtis. Either way, it meant people were watching devotedly.

But work was only a small part of Isabelle's delight that summer. Far more wonderful was the time she and Michael spent together outside the studio. He took her out on romantic evenings, and other times they stayed home, comfortable, lazy and happy just to be with each other. Their lovemaking was passionate, but equally important to Isabelle were their long evenings spent talking and enjoying each other's company.

They often took Jenny with them on an afternoon's ramble through the park or out for a burger and children's movie or to Disneyland or the beach. Even the silly disguises Michael and Isabelle sometimes had to adopt to keep from being recognized and mobbed were a source of amusement. Michael was wonderful with Jenny, accepting her limitations calmly, but never patronizing her. Jenny, in return, was crazy about him. Whenever he wasn't around, she asked about him, and when he was there, she was stuck like glue to his side, talking, and holding his hand, showing him what she had made or learned.

Watching them together, Isabelle's heart swelled with love and pride. She did not speak of love to Michael; she felt a superstitious fear that she would somehow spoil it all if she told him that she had fallen madly, deeply in love with him again. If the truth were told, she knew, she loved him more now than she had ten years ago, for she loved him, not with the giddy, easy crush of a teenager, but with the heart of a woman, deepened by pain and experience.

But then one day at the beach, as they sat on the sand watching Jenny build a sand castle, with Isabelle sitting snugly between Michael's legs, her back against his chest and his arms around her, he bent and kissed her shoulder, murmuring, "I love you."

Suddenly it became the easiest thing in the world for her to reply, "I love you, too."

Isabelle turned her head to look at him, her eyes sparkling with tears. His eyebrows rose a little. "What? That makes you cry?"

She swallowed back her tears, smiling, and shook her head. "Just with happiness."

"Surely you must have guessed."

"I hoped. I knew I loved you, but I was afraid to say it. Like it would break the spell."

He grinned. "Nothing's going to break it. Don't worry." He kissed the tip of her nose playfully and squeezed her to him.

But Isabelle, turning back to gaze out at Jenny and the ocean beyond her, could not be as sure as he was. There was a dark worm of doubt that nibbled away at her happiness, for she had not told him that Jenny was his daughter.

She should have revealed it long ago, she knew. Nancy had told her so in no uncertain terms a couple of weeks earlier when Isabelle had confided her problem to her. But Isabelle had not been able to bring herself to do it. Though her fears that Michael would reject Jenny or not be a good father for her were obviously unfounded, she had been unable to shake the fear that he would eventually leave them. His departure would be even more crushing to Jenny, she thought, if she knew that Michael was her father.

She had struggled over her duty to protect Jenny and her duty to tell Michael that Jenny was his child for so long that finally she realized that even if she told him now, Michael was bound to be angry with her for not telling him sooner. *What if he stormed out of her life because he was furious over her deception?* Every day that she waited made it harder and harder to reveal the truth. Several times she worked up her courage to tell him, but then something would happen that would distract her, or the words would stick in her throat.

So she let the days slide by without telling Michael about Jenny, hoping that somehow she would find a safe way to do it. But that way never seemed to come.

Two weeks after that day at the beach, Isabelle was surprised when she heard her doorbell ring and looked out to find Michael on the doorstep. They had not planned to see each other tonight, one of the rare evenings when they didn't. Michael was leaving the following morning on a four-day tour of the Northwest, arranged by the studio's publicity department, and Isabelle had a heavy shooting schedule tomorrow.

"Michael!" She swung the door open, smiling, all thought of memorizing her lines tonight receding in the joy she always felt at seeing him. "What are you doing here?"

He grabbed her and swung her around, then pulled her close for an enthusiastic kiss. When he released her, Isabelle was breathless.

"What in the world—" she gasped. "What's going on?"

"Going on?" he asked with an air of mock innocence. "What makes you think anything is going on?"

Isabelle grimaced. "Come on, don't make me drag it
out of you."

"You see before you," he said gravely, stepping back
and assuming the stance of an old-fashioned orator, his
hand hooked in a nonexistent coat lapel, "a man who is
going to read for the lead role in a prime-time series."

Isabelle's jaw dropped. "Michael! Oh, Michael, that's
wonderful!" She threw herself back into his arms,
wrapping her arms around his neck and squeezing hard.

Finally she released him and stepped back. "So tell me.
Give me all the details."

"It looks good. Amon Hatcher Productions is producing it, so you know it's got a good chance of being
bought."

"Michael! That's great! When do you read for it?
Aren't you excited?"

"Walking on air would be more like it," he grinned.
"The audition is next Tuesday, right after I get back. By
that time, of course, I'll be sick with terror, but right now
I'm having a hard time staying off the ceiling. My agent
just called me. I've got to run over to his house and pick
up the script, but first I had to come by and tell you."

"I'm glad." Isabelle beamed at him. "You'll get it—I
know you will. You're too good an actor not to."

"An unbiased opinion." He laughed, his eyes dancing.

"Just because I happen to love you doesn't mean I
don't know what's good," she retorted.

"Michael!" Jenny came into the room, and her eyes lit
up at seeing him.

"Jenny! How's my girl? Come give me a hug."

Jenny was more than happy to comply, running over and throwing her arms around his waist. "Mama said you weren't coming tonight."

"I hadn't planned to."

"But he had great news, so he came to tell us," Isabelle explained.

"Really?" Jenny's eyes grew huge and round. "What?"

"I have an audition for a role. A nighttime series."

"Oh." Jenny was clearly less impressed by the news than they were. "Is that good?"

Michael chuckled. "Yes, sweetheart. It's very good."

"I'm glad." Jenny threw her arms around him for another hug, then stepped back. "You want to see what I made in school today?" Jenny's school ran year-round, so even though it was summer, she still went to school half a day.

"Sure. I'd love to."

Michael and Isabelle waited, smiling, as Jenny ran back to her room. She returned a moment later, carefully carrying a circular, almost flat, piece of fired clay. Isabelle had already seen it. It was an impression of Jenny's hand, which had then been painted and fired. She made one every year, marking on it her name and age.

Suddenly Isabelle's stomach turned to ice. *Jenny's age! He would know when he saw that!* She waited, frozen; there was nothing she could do to stop Michael from taking the hand, as he was doing, and looking at it.

"Wonderful!"

"We do one every year," Jenny volunteered.

"I see. So you can see how much your hand has grown?"

Jenny nodded, pleased that he understood. Isabelle took a step forward, saying, "Jenny, why don't you take the plate and—"

"I want to give it to him," Jenny countered. Isabelle's heart sank.

"Why, thank you, Jenny." Michael smiled, looking down at the hand impression again. His eyes fell to the bottom of the plate. He went very still.

Slowly he raised his head and looked straight at Isabelle. "Ten?" he asked hoarsely. "Jenny is ten?"

"In April," Jenny happily supplied. "I was ten in April."

Michael glanced at her, then back at Isabelle. "Then she's—"

Isabelle nodded, stiffening her spine.

Twelve

―――――

"Jenny..." Isabelle said quietly. "Why don't you go back to your room now and look at the TV show you were watching? Okay?"

"Okay." Jenny looked disappointed, but then turned to Michael and took his hand. "You come, too. It's that show—" She made a vague gesture with her hands. "He says, 'And now let's see what Mr. Bear is doing.'" She imitated a grown man's syrupy voice.

"Another time, sweetheart." Michael was pale, and his voice was still as death. "Right now I have to talk to your mother."

His eyes followed Jenny as she went down the hall to her bedroom. Then he turned back to Isabelle.

"She's mine?" His words fell like rocks between them.

"Yes."

There was a long moment of silence. Michael shook his head. "Good God, why didn't you tell me?"

"You had left me. I didn't even know your address."

"You could have called. Did you make any effort to find me?" He scowled at her darkly.

"No!" Isabelle shot back, lifting her chin. "I saw no reason to. You had left me. You obviously didn't want anything to do with me. Why would I think you had any interest in my child, either?"

"You know why I left. But a baby would have made it an entirely different situation."

"You think I would try to hold you by using my baby?" Isabelle replied scornfully. "All I knew was that you had dropped me flat. That you hadn't even waited to say goodbye to me in person, just left me a note and took off. Do you think I would call you and beg you to come back because I was pregnant?"

"No, you're too full of stubborn, stupid pride! Damn!" Michael thrust his hands back into his hair. "All those years lost—all that time I was a father and didn't even know it!"

"I had to do what I thought was best—for me and for my baby. I had enough problems without worrying about whether I was doing you a disservice by not telling you!"

Michael turned and began to pace distractedly up and down the room. "Hell, Isabelle..." He paused and turned to her. "I guess I can understand why you didn't tell me when you knew you were pregnant. But—" he faced her squarely, his voice hardening "—why in the hell didn't you tell me when I came here? After I explained to you about my leaving and you'd forgiven me, why didn't you tell me? You knew how much I had wanted a child. You could see how much I liked Jenny. Why didn't you tell me?"

"Because I was scared!"

"Scared! Of what! Me?"

"At first I didn't tell you because I didn't know how you'd react to Jenny. I told you that I'd known men before who didn't want her around."

"You couldn't have thought I didn't like her!"

"No. Once I saw you with her, I knew you weren't like that. You were good with her, and—but there was still the chance that you'd leave, that you and I would find out we didn't have the same feelings anymore, and then you'd leave. It would have hurt Jenny doubly if she had known that you were her father. I—I wanted to protect her."

"From me?" His blue eyes flashed. "You thought that I would have abandoned my daughter! Is that what you think of me? That I'm a callous son of a bitch with no real feelings? That I'd drop Jenny like a hot potato as soon as I wasn't in your bed?"

"No, of course not," Isabelle began.

"Then what did you think?"

"I don't know—I'm not sure. The longer it went on, the harder it was to tell you. I was afraid you'd be angry with me, just like you are! I was scared to do anything to upset the relationship. It was too wonderful to risk it. I'm sorry, Michael. I didn't mean to hurt you. I didn't want to hide it from you. I just...put it off, and then it got worse and worse the longer I didn't say anything. Can't you understand?"

"Yeah, I understand." His voice was laced with bitterness. "I understand that you didn't trust me enough to tell me the truth. I understand that you've been deceiving me all these months, hiding secrets from me. What else is there that I don't know about?"

"Nothing!" Isabelle flared. "Michael, please, don't be like this."

"How else should I be? What should I do? Just say, 'Oh, sure, I don't mind that you didn't tell me that Jenny

is my daughter. It's okay that I'm in love with you and
you say you're in love with me, and yet you kept this se
cret from me? What does it matter that you've been ly
ing to me all this time?' I'm sorry, but I can't do that."

"I didn't lie to you!"

"You sure as hell didn't tell me the truth! You think
you're absolved because I didn't ask you a direct ques
tion, 'Is Jenny my daughter?'"

"No." Isabelle turned aside. Her heart ached within
her. *Had she lost him forever? Was Michael too angry,
too hurt, to forgive her?* "I was wrong. I should have told
you. I'm sorry."

"I want Jenny to know that I'm her father. I want to
be a father to her."

Isabelle nodded, not looking at him. "All right." She
wanted to ask him, "And what about us?" but she found
that she didn't have the nerve. She didn't want to hear
him say that it was over between them.

"But not now," she went on quietly. "I don't think
either of us is in the proper mood to tell her something
like that."

"You're right." His voice was heavy. Isabelle braved a
glance at him. He looked weary and hard. He glanced
around the room in a kind of stunned way, almost as if
he didn't know the place. "I have to go now. I have to
think. I'll talk to you later."

Isabelle wanted to cry and beg him to forgive her, but
pride kept her knees stiff and her back straight, at least
until he was out the door. Then she sank down onto the
floor right where she was, the strength she had sum
moned up now vanished, and she gave way to her tears.

Isabelle dragged herself through the next few days. She
looked and felt so awful the next day that the director had

finally cut short the filming. The weekend was no improvement. Though she did not have to cope with her job, she had plenty of free time to think—and that was just as bad. She was afraid that she had lost Michael for good. He did not phone her, even though she did not leave the house all weekend, just so she would be by the telephone in case he did. And she could not call him to apologize, since he was on tour and she didn't know exactly where he was. Not, she reminded herself, that apologizing would make any difference. Michael certainly hadn't seemed swayed by her apologies the other night.

He was furious, and Isabelle was honest enough to know that he had reason to be. She should have told him weeks ago. Now that she thought about it, really thought about it, she was not sure why she had not. It had been a difficult thing to do, but that didn't explain away her reluctance to tell him; she had faced up to lots of other things that she did not enjoy and had done them. *Why was this so different?*

The answer came to her in the feeling in the pit of her stomach. She was afraid—afraid of losing Michael again, afraid of giving herself completely to him and once again being left behind, heartbroken. It had been so painful when he left the first time, and it had been made even harder by the discovery that she was pregnant. Then, after Jenny's birth, she had struggled through months of fear and pain, worrying about whether Jenny would even survive. It had been the most terrible time of her life.

To protect herself against the pain, she had built up a wall. Looking back, she could see now how she had refused to let anyone else in, except for her mother and father. She had dated rarely, and when she did, the relationship never lasted for long. For ten years, she had

not let herself care for another man, commit to anothe
man. It had been easy to pretend that she did it to pro
tect Jenny, when in reality she was the one who ha
wanted the protection.

Then, when Michael came back into her life, she ha
been unable to keep him out. She had fallen in love wit
him all over again. But she had been reluctant to giv
herself to him, heart and soul. Keeping the knowledg
from him that he was Jenny's father had been her last
ditch defense. Somehow it represented a separation fron
him, a barrier, as if she could keep her heart safe by hid
ing this secret from him.

But when he walked out on her, everything had crashe
down on her. She realized then that she had not been abl
to keep her heart safe; she loved him too much. And al
she had wound up doing was hurting them both. Isa
belle hated herself for what she had done. She had bee
both a coward and a fool. Worse, she might very wel
have destroyed all hope for happiness for her and Mi
chael.

She wished she could explain to him, apologize, let him
know how very much she loved him. But there was an ic
knot forming in her chest as each day passed with no
word from Michael. She began to be afraid that she
would never get the opportunity to even try to set thing
right.

Isabelle leaned back against the couch in the actors
lounge. Her head and neck ached, and there was still an
other scene to shoot. This was, she thought the mos
miserable Monday of her life. Michael should be com
ing home today, with the other actor and publicists who
had gone on the tour, and Isabelle had been both eage

nd sick with fear all day long. She felt as if her very life
vere hanging in the balance.

Felice plopped down on the couch beside her and eased
er feet out of her shoes. "These blasted heels," she
rumbled, rubbing one of her feet. "I think Wardrobe
urposely gets the highest, thinnest heels they can find for
ne. Amanda hates me."

"Oh, Felice..." Isabelle smiled faintly.

"She does. Ever since the time last year when I re-
used to wear that awful olive-green dress she got for me.
)o you remember?"

Isabelle's smile grew broader. "I remember the fight."

"It made me look like a cow, a sick one at that." She
aused, then said thoughtfully, "Do you suppose she's
ctually getting shoes that are a half size too small for
ne?"

Isabelle couldn't hold back a chuckle.

"Well, at least I got a laugh out of you. You've looked
ike gloom-and-doom lately." Felice swung around to
ace Isabelle, pulling her legs up and sitting cross-legged,
eedless of her long taffeta skirt. "I guess it's 'cause Mi-
hael's been gone, huh?"

"I guess."

"It's pretty exciting about his audition, isn't it?"

"What?" Isabelle dragged her attention back to Fe-
ice. *How did the show's grapevine always manage to
vork so effectively?* "Yes, it is."

"I'm sure Danny will be furious if Michael gets the
ob." Felice shrugged and grinned. "That ought to teach
)anny not to be so tight. It's his fault for signing Mi-
hael to only a one-year contract. I mean, a guy like Mi-
hael, what does he expect?"

Isabelle nodded. "Yeah, it'll work out just right if the
etwork picks up the series."

They would shoot the pilot for airing next spring, an
if the network picked it up for the fall season, filmin
would probably begin about the time Michael's contrac
was up. It would be a perfect situation for him.

Isabelle wanted very much for him to get the role—i
was most soap actors' dream to move into prime time o
even better, movies. But she couldn't entirely get rid o
the ache in her chest at the thought of not seeing hir
every day on the set. If he decided to break off their re
lationship, then it would mean that she would never se
him at all. Her heart twisted inside her at the thought.

"There's Tish." Felice waved to the AD standing in th
doorway of the lounge and unfolded her legs. "Time t
get back to the salt mines." She shoved her feet into he
shoes, grimacing as she did so. "Come on, let's get thi
scene over with so we can all go home."

"Yeah." Isabelle rose and followed Felice and Tish t
the set, where two of the other actors were already wait
ing for them, as well as the makeup artist to do the last
minute touch-ups.

The scene went quickly. They were all competent ac
tors and eager to get through for the day. When the scen
was over, they all relaxed, Felice with a groan of relief a
she quickly bent and pulled off her offending shoes. Is
abelle turned to walk off the set.

There, standing just inside the door, was Michael. Is
abelle stopped. Her heart began to race, and she fel
suddenly cold, then hot, then cold again.

The other actors greeted him as they filed out the doo
Isabelle just stood, unable to move her feet forward. Mi
chael looked at her. He stuck his hands in his pockets an
looked down at his feet, then back up at her. He tried t
smile.

'Too mad to even talk to me?" he asked finally.

"Oh, Michael." Isabelle went toward him in a rush. He moved forward, too, his arms held out, and enveloped her in a hug.

Isabelle's arms went tightly around his waist, and she laid her head against his chest. His chest was hard and warm beneath her face, his heartbeat reassuringly steady. She could feel his lips brush her hair.

"I'm sorry, sweetheart. I'm sorry," he whispered.

Tears sprang into Isabelle's eyes and trickled out. Her heart felt as if it might burst with joy. "Oh, Michael."

He chuckled huskily. "Can't you say anything else?"

"No. Yes." She raised her head and looked up at him. "I'm so happy to see you. I was sure you would hate me forever."

He bent and pressed his lips to her forehead, then her nose and finally her mouth. "I could never hate you."

Isabelle let out a breathy little laugh. "I'll hold you to that."

"Come on, let's get out of here," Michael said, glancing over at the crew, interestedly watching.

Arms around each other, they walked down the hall to Isabelle's dressing room, and Isabelle locked the door firmly behind them.

"When'd you get back?" she asked.

"About forty minutes ago."

She raised her eyebrows quizzically at him. Michael looked a little sheepish.

"I drove straight here," he admitted. "I didn't want to talk to you on the phone about it, so I couldn't call you, and—oh, hell! I was torn up inside. I missed you so much."

Isabelle went into his arms again, flinging her arms around his neck and kissing him. "I missed you, too," she whispered when she finally pulled her mouth away.

"I thought you didn't call because you were mad at me. I was afraid I'd lost you forever. I was so wrong and so stupid not to tell you earlier! I'm sorry. I'm so sorry."

He shook his head and squeezed her to him tightly, laying his cheek against her hair. "We all screw up. Believe me, I ought to know. I did it ten years ago with you. I understand why you didn't tell me. I was hurt and angry, but when I calmed down and thought about it, it made sense. I mean, I had let you down terribly before. I told myself all these years that I had left you for your own good, but, you know, maybe I was just running scared. Loving you threatened the life I had planned for myself. It was too big, too much responsibility, and I was too young and scared and stupid to handle it. I should have thought about the possibility of your being pregnant. I should have asked you. I should have stayed there and talked to you face-to-face. But I took the coward's way out. I ran back to New York, and I didn't even let myself think about the fact that you might have gotten pregnant. You were right to be angry with me. And I've given up my right to be told about Jenny, taking off like that."

"No." Isabelle shook her head firmly. "No, you didn't. No matter what happened, you were her father then, and you still are, and you don't have to deserve it. It's just there, a fact, and you should have been told about it."

He smiled. "Now are we going to argue about this?"

Isabelle smiled and shook her head. "I don't plan to argue with you at all tonight. I'm too happy to have you back."

"Me, too. Anyway, I thought it all out, and I realized, sure, maybe you should have told me earlier that Jenny was mine. But I could understand why you hadn't and why it had been harder and harder to tell me after that. And you were right to protect Jenny from the possibility of my hurting her. How were you to know I wouldn't take off again? Most important, I realized that if I stayed mad, if I pouted and stayed away from you, I'd only be hurting myself. I love you. I want to be with you. I want to be Jenny's father. To hell with being upset because I didn't know four months ago. I know *now*, and I want to enjoy it."

Isabelle gazed lovingly into his eyes. "Has anyone ever told you what a really great, wonderful, stupendous man you are?"

He grinned. "Not today."

"Well, you are."

"Good. Then I can assume that when I ask you to marry me, you'll say yes?"

"What!" Isabelle stared at him, stunned. "Marry you!"

"Well, yes. How else am I going to live with you and be a father to Jenny and have the rest of the family I want? I want to marry you. I want you to be my wife. Will you?"

"Yes. Oh, yes!" Isabelle didn't hesitate. She flung herself into his arms again. He lifted her and spun her around, both of them laughing with excitement and joy.

Finally, when he set her down again and they kissed each other enough times to seal their engagement, Michael pulled away and said, "Come on. Get out of those clothes, and let's pick up Jenny and tell her the news. Then we're going to celebrate."

Isabelle couldn't stop grinning as she quickly skimmed out of her costume and into her own shorts and top. She slathered on cream to remove her makeup and playfully smeared some of it on Michael's face. "Here, you'd better use it, too. I've gotten lipstick and makeup all over you."

Grumbling a little, Michael wiped it off while Isabelle completed her larger task of taking off the heavy makeup she wore for filming.

"But, you know, Michael," she said, her voice turning serious, "we better not spend too long tonight celebrating. Your audition's tomorrow morning, isn't it?"

He shook his head. "No. I'm not auditioning."

"What?" Isabelle turned and stared at him. "Why not?"

"When I got the script from my agent, he told me that it's going to be filmed primarily in New Orleans. That's where it takes place, and the producer wants the gritty realism of Bourbon Street, et cetera."

"Oh."

"So I told him to forget it. Why audition? I'm not moving to New Orleans and leaving you and Jenny here. And you two couldn't go with me. I mean, there's your job, and Jenny needs to stay with her school."

"But, Michael—"

"No. No 'buts.' That job is not what I want. I'm not leaving you again for any role."

Tears welled in Isabelle's eyes and threatened to spill over. Her heart felt as if it were about to burst with love. Still, she made one last attempt. "But your career...."

Michael made a brief, inelegant remark concerning his career, and Isabelle chuckled.

"There will be other roles," he assured her. "But this is the only life I've got, and I want it to be right here and right now with you and my daughter."

Isabelle smiled radiantly and stretched up to kiss him. "Then what are we waiting for? Let's go tell Jenny that she has a father."

* * * * * *

SILHOUETTE®
Desire®

COMING NEXT MONTH

#967 A COWBOY CHRISTMAS—Ann Major

Born under the same Christmas star, December's *Man of the Month,* Leander Knight, and sexy Heddy Kinney shared the same destiny. Now the handsome cowboy had to stop her holiday wedding—to *another* man!

#968 MIRACLES AND MISTLETOE—Cait London

Rugged cowboy Jonah Fargo was a Scrooge when it came to Christmas—until Harmony Davis sauntered into his life. Could she get him under the mistletoe and make him believe in miracles?

#969 COWBOYS DON'T STAY—Anne McAllister

Code of the West

Tess Montgomery had fallen for Noah Tanner years ago, but he left her with a broken heart *and* a baby. Now that he was back, could he convince her that sometimes cowboys do stay?

#970 CHRISTMAS WEDDING—Pamela Macaluso

Just Married

Holly Bryant was expected to pose as Jesse Tyler's bride-to-be, not fall for the hardheaded man! But Jesse was a woman's dream come true, even though he swore he'd never settle down....

#971 TEXAS PRIDE—Barbara McCauley

Hearts of Stone

Jessica Stone didn't need help from anyone, especially a lone wolf like Dylan Grant. But Dylan refused to let Jessica's Texas pride—and her to-die-for looks—stand in his way!

#972 GIFT WRAPPED DAD—Sandra Steffen

Six-year-old Tommy Wilson asked Santa for a dad, so he was thrilled when Will Sutherland showed up in time for Christmas. Now if only Will could convince Tommy's mom he'd make the perfect husband for her!

CHRISTMAS WEDDING
by Pamela Macaluso

Don't miss JUST MARRIED, a fun-filled miniseries by Pamela Macaluso about three men with wealth, power and looks to die for. These bad boys had everything—except the love of a good woman.

***

"Will you pretend *to be my fiancée?"* Holly Bryant knew millionaire Jesse Tyler was the most eligible bachelor around—not that a hunk with attitude was her idea of husband material. But then, she and Jesse weren't really engaged, and his steamy mistletoe kisses were just part of the charade...weren't they?

Find out in *Christmas Wedding,* book three of the JUST MARRIED series, coming to you in December... only from

SILHOUETTE®

Desire®

Hearts of Stone

Three strong-willed Texas siblings whose rock-hard protective walls are about to come tumblin' down!

The Silhouette Desire miniseries by

BARBARA McCAULEY

concludes in December 1995 with

TEXAS PRIDE (Silhouette Desire #971)

Raised with a couple of overprotective brothers, Jessica Stone *hated* to be told what to do. So when her sexy new foreman started trying to run her life, Jessica's pride said she had to put a stop to it. But her heart said something *entirely* different....

HOS3

SILHOUETTE® Desire®

ANGELS AND ELVES
by Joan Elliott Pickart

Joan Elliott Pickart brings you her special brand of humor tales of the MacAllister men. For these carefree bachelors, predicting the particulars of the MacAllister babies is much easier than predicting when wedding bells will sound!

In November, Silhouette Desire's *Man of the Month,* Forrest MacAllister, is the reigning Baby Bet Champion and a confirmed "uncle." Until his very pregnant, matchmaking sister introduced him to Jillian Jones-Jenkins, he never would have thought that the next baby he bets on might be his own!

Experience all the laughter and love as a new MacAllister baby is born, and the most unpredictable MacAllister becomes a husband—and father in *Angels and Elves,* book one of THE BABY BET.

In February 1996, Silhouette Special Edition celebrates the most romantic month of the year with FRIENDS, LOVERS...AND BABIES! book two of THE BABY BET.

Three brothers…
Three proud, strong men who live—and love—by

THE CODE OF THE WEST

Meet the Tanner brothers—Robert, Luke, and now, Noah—in Anne McAllister's

COWBOYS DON'T STAY
(December, Desire #969)

Tess Montgomery had fallen for Noah Tanner years ago—but he left her with a broken heart *and* a baby. Now he was back, but could he convince her that sometimes cowboys do stay?

Only from